FATAL MARRIAGE

CHARLOTTE BYRD

CHARLOTTE BYRD

dangerously addictive

Identifiers

ISBN (e-book): 978-1-63225-113-8

ISBN (paperback):978-1-63225-114-5

❊ Created with Vellum

ABOUT FATAL MARRIAGE (WEDLOCKED TRILOGY BOOK 3)

I was forced into this marriage to save my father's life and our family's empire, but my husband has other plans.

He wants to sell Tate Media for parts and make himself billions in the process.

The only way I can stop him is to expose his not-so-secret life.

Franklin Parks is a **monster.** We have all heard the rumors, but anyone who has dared to stand up to him has been silenced. Now, it's my turn.

He is protected by all of the rich and powerful because he protects their secrets in return.

There's only person I can trust: Henry Asher, the love of my life.

I shouldn't get him involved. It's too dangerous, but we can't stay away from each other.

Can I escape my marriage and save my legacy or will I lose everything and everyone I love in the process?

What readers are saying about Charlotte Byrd's Books:

"This book/series is addictive! Super hot and steamy, intense with twists and turns in the plot that you just won't see coming…" ★★★★★

"One-sitting read!" ★★★★★

"How on earth did I survive that? **My mind is blown,** my hearts beating out of my chest and I'm on this cliff, shaking like a leaf in a windstorm waiting to do that all over again with the conclusion to one of the best reasons to get out of work and get lost for a while." ★★★★★

"This series is just so **intense and delicious.** The stunning twists, raw emotions and nerve wracking tension just keep increasing as each book in this enticing series unfolds. I am so invested in Nicholas and Olivia. These characters really worm their way into your heart, while also totally consuming your mind. The gripping story quickly captivates and pulls you back into this couple's world. Do try to be prepared for the cliffhanger and the wait for the sixth and final book in this amazing series."

keeps you riding on the edge the whole series. You'll love it!" ★★★★★

"What is Love Worth. This is a great epic ending to this series. Nicholas and Olive have a deep connection and the mystery surrounding the deaths of the people he is accused of murdering is to be read. Olive is one strong woman with deep convictions. The twists, angst, confusion is all put together to make this worthwhile read."
★★★★★

"Fast-paced romantic suspense filled with twists and turns, danger, betrayal, and so much more."
★★★★★

"Decadent, delicious, & dangerously addictive!" - Amazon Review ★★★★★

"Titillation so masterfully woven, no reader can resist its pull. A MUST-BUY!" - Bobbi Koe, Amazon Review ★★★★★

"Captivating!" - Crystal Jones, Amazon Review
★★★★★

"Sexy, secretive, pulsating chemistry…" - Mrs. K, Amazon Reviewer ★★★★★

"Charlotte Byrd is a brilliant writer. I've read loads and I've laughed and cried. She writes a balanced book with brilliant characters. Well done!" - Amazon Review ★★★★★

"Hot, steamy, and a great storyline." - Christine Reese ★★★★★

"My oh my....Charlotte has made me a fan for life." - JJ, Amazon Reviewer ★★★★★

"Wow. Just wow. Charlotte Byrd leaves me speechless and humble… It definitely kept me on the edge of my seat. Once you pick it up, you won't put it down." - Amazon Review ★★★★★

" Intrigue, lust, and great characters...what more could you ask for?!" - Dragonfly Lady ★★★★★

WANT TO BE THE FIRST TO KNOW ABOUT MY UPCOMING SALES, NEW RELEASES AND EXCLUSIVE GIVEAWAYS?

Sign up for my newsletter: https://www. subscribepage.com/byrdVIPList

Join my Facebook Group: https://www.facebook. com/groups/276340079439433/

Bonus Points: Follow me on BookBub and Goodreads!

ABOUT CHARLOTTE BYRD

Charlotte Byrd is the bestselling author of romantic suspense novels. She has sold over 600,000 books and has been translated into five languages.

She lives near Palm Springs, California with her husband, son, and a toy Australian Shepherd who hates water. Charlotte is addicted to books and Netflix and she loves hot weather and crystal blue water.

Write her here:

charlotte@charlotte-byrd.com

Check out her books here:

www.charlotte-byrd.com

Connect with her here:

www.facebook.com/charlottebyrdbooks

www.instagram.com/charlottebyrdbooks

www.twitter.com/byrdauthor

Want to hear about new releases, free books and get exclusive giveaways?

Sign up for my newsletter!

Sign up for my newsletter: https://www.subscribepage.com/byrdVIPList

Join my Facebook Group: https://www.facebook.com/groups/276340079439433/

Bonus Points: Follow me on BookBub and Goodreads!

facebook.com/charlottebyrdbooks

twitter.com/byrdauthor

instagram.com/charlottebyrdbooks

bookbub.com/profile/charlotte-byrd

Tell Me to Stop
Tell Me to Go
Tell Me to Stay
Tell Me to Run
Tell Me to Fight
Tell Me to Lie

Tangled Series

Tangled up in Ice
Tangled up in Pain
Tangled up in Lace
Tangled up in Hate
Tangled up in Love

Black Series

Black Edge
Black Rules
Black Bounds
Black Contract
Black Limit

Lavish Trilogy

Lavish Lies
Lavish Betrayal
Lavish Obsession

Standalone Novels

Debt

Offer

Unknown

Dressing Mr. Dalton

1

AURORA

I should have handled that better. Henry and I had a beautiful night where we made amends. We made promises and yet when I went to see my father, it all went out of the window. It's as if none of that ever happened. At least, that's what he must think but it's not true.

I love him as much as I ever loved him. He is the only man who will forever have my heart and he is the one man who should never worry about whether or not he is the one.

Yet, here I am, about to walk down the aisle and marry someone else.

I owe him an explanation. I know that.

Of course I do.

Yet, I'm afraid that if I were to see him, then I couldn't go through with this.

The following morning, I get ready as if I'm getting ready for war. My makeup and my wedding dress are my armor and this marriage is a battle that I have to win. I sit in front of the vanity for a long time, completely alone, steadying myself for what is about to come.

For most brides, this is the happiest moment in their lives but not for me. I don't know what to expect but I know that it won't be good.

The one thing that I know for sure is that I am no longer just doing it for my father. I'm doing it for all of those people who worked for Tate Media.

They deserve better.

I need to be able to save their retirements.

I need to be able to protect the company that is rightfully mine.

When my mom comes in, I tell her that I need some time alone. I don't want to see anyone. I want to do this entirely myself. I even kick out the photographer.

I put on some music and carefully apply a layer of foundation followed by winged eyeliner and a coat of mascara. When tears start to well up and a big gulp forms at the back of my throat, I take a few deep breaths to push the pain away.

My thoughts return to Henry.

This should be him who I am marrying. I think back to his dark hair and his beautiful wide eyes.

I imagine him standing at the end of the aisle, waiting for me to walk into his arms. I imagine what it would be like to spend the rest of my life with him and I know that I would be very happy.

I remember what it was like the last time that he held me in his arms and how safe and protected I felt. I want him to protect me now, but I don't think that he can. I have already put his life in danger just by telling him what I told him and I don't want to make things worse.

"Get a hold of yourself," I say out loud while tears stream down my cheeks and my mascara makes black puddles around my eyes.

For a moment I let myself go.

If I keep it in too much and if I hide my feelings away from me, then I'm afraid that they will come out at the worst possible time, like during the wedding.

"No. Cry now and then get a hold of yourself," I say.

The tears that started out as little pearls have

morphed into thick wide drops that cover my face and neck.

I thought it would be easier to stop if I got everything out of my system but somehow the floodgates have opened and now my emotions are completely uncontrollable.

"What are you doing?" Ellis says, after bursting into the room.

The photographer is close behind her.

I try to wipe my face but it's all to no avail.

"Don't you know that you can't cry like that? It's going to make your face all puffy and red. No amount of makeup is going to be able to cover it up. Do you want to look terrible in your wedding pictures?"

"Well, that would at least be an accurate portrayal," I say sarcastically.

She applies some ice from her glass to my eyes.

"I don't know why you're so upset with this," Ellis says. "He is the most eligible bachelor in New York and he's actually interested in marrying you."

"Well, thanks for that," I mumble.

"No. I didn't mean it like that."

"Well, you know what I mean."

"No, actually I don't."

"My parents run one of the biggest media empires in the world and I'm supposed to be…"

My voice trails just as I realize that she doesn't know that I am being coerced into this marriage. "What are you saying exactly?" I turn toward her. "That I don't deserve him?"

"Of course not. I'm just saying that he's a great catch and you are lucky to have him. You are both lucky to have each other." Ellis corrects herself.

I don't believe her and frankly, I wish she wasn't here but it would've been more complicated not to invite her since I have known her since I was in school.

The only person that I want to see right now besides Henry is Karlie, the girl that I met at the bridal shop. She'd turned out to be an old friend of mine from middle school. We reconnected and we told each other some truths, the kind that I could never tell Ellis or any of my other friends.

I invited her to the wedding and she said that she would come but the last time we talked I got the sense that she knew something was off with my relationship with Franklin.

No one but Henry knows the truth about why I'm doing this and even he only knows a portion. After our night together, I was so certain that I would be able to talk to my father and convince him that I did not have to do this.

Little did I know that my father would drop a bombshell into my lap. His life is in danger and the only way he will be safe is for me to marry Franklin, the only man that can protect him.

I went over there trying to get out and I only got myself further in.

"Okay," Ellis says, taking a step away from me. "I think that you're ready now."

She turns my chair around and I look at myself in the mirror. She did a good job. The tears are gone and so is the darkness under my eyes. Even the puffiness has disappeared.

I look beautiful but incredibly sad. I force a smile but that seems to only draw attention to the sorrow in my eyes.

2

AURORA

Ellis turns her attention to my hair. I was going to do this myself but I'm afraid that if I were to be alone again, I wouldn't be able to stop the tears.

It's good to have her here; she's a distraction that I desperately need.

Ellis talks about the guy that she's seeing and I'm not following along. He's one in a long line and I'm sure that there will be others after him.

"I think that I'm going to marry him," she says.

I look up at her and raise my eyebrows.

"Really?" I ask, surprised.

"I love him, well, as much as I can love anyone. He's not a Birkin bag, you know." She laughs and I laugh.

She says that she's just kidding but we both know that she's not.

"What makes you say that?" I ask.

"Well, I like spending time with him. He's smart, charming, runs in the same social circle."

"But are you in love with him?" I ask.

"What does that matter?"

"Isn't that the reason to get married?"

"I don't know, Aurora, is it?" she asks me.

I narrow my eyes trying to figure out what she does or doesn't know.

"What are you referring to?"

"I don't know," she says, holding her arms across her chest. "You just don't seem to be that into Franklin. It's almost as if this whole relationship, or engagement, or wedding wasn't your idea."

"I don't know," I say as innocently as possible. "It's not that I don't care about Franklin but this is more his idea than mine."

"You're still hung up on Henry, aren't you?" Ellis asks. "Do you know that most people think that this doesn't work and that women are forced to marry men for a variety of circumstances? Even if they're not full-on coerced, there are always other considerations besides love when it comes to marriage. Especially if you are from established families like we are."

"What are you talking about? Your mother has had a number of husbands and she has all of her own money."

"Yes, people think that we have money but perception isn't always reality."

I tilt my head and wait for her to explain.

"We don't have as much money as we should. My mother has made a lot of really, really, really bad investments. In fact, she's filing bankruptcy and we are probably going to lose all of the properties. David, the guy that I'm dating now, has a lot to offer me and he loves me. If he were to ask me, how could I say no?"

As I walk down the aisle toward Franklin, my thoughts are no longer on just my predicament but also on Ellis's and all of those hundreds of thousands of women out there who have to marry men they don't love just to keep their position in life.

People say that money isn't everything, but sometimes it's the only thing.

If my father had run his company in the proper way and not squandered the whole pension fund and hadn't made bad investments that left him practically bankrupt, then I wouldn't be doing this to not only save my legacy but also all of those innocent people's lives who would be ruined if they lost the only money they had.

There was a moment when I thought that I could get out of it. I thought that I could be selfish and just run away and start my life with Henry but now, I know that I have to go through with it. I have to jump into the fire in order to make everything right again. There are no guarantees but I have to try.

When I take my position next to Franklin at the altar, I repeat the vows that the minister says but instead of that promise, I make myself another.

I vow to save Tate Media and to take control of it, I say silently to myself. I vow that nothing like this will ever happen again.

After we exchange our vows and the choir sings their praises and everyone at the church stands up and claps as we walk out, I glance over at Franklin and feel sick to my stomach.

He looks genuinely happy.

Despite everything that's happened, I suddenly have a doubt about whether I'm wrong about him.

Maybe he has his faults but what if he actually loves me? Is that possible?

No matter how attractive he is or how charming, I have to remember the truth.

He knows full well that I have agreed to marry him under certain circumstances and he is enforcing them. He knows that I don't love him and he clearly doesn't love me.

In fact, he barely even respects me. If he did, then I wouldn't have caught him in bed with another woman when we were still trying to make things work.

I have never been intimate with him and as I dance with him on the dance floor in front of all of these strangers, I wonder what will happen tonight.

I don't want to sleep with him but it's our wedding night.

Will he take no for an answer?

WE SAY goodbye to our guests around two in the morning. I want to stay out even longer but everyone starts to disperse. I say goodbye to my father last and we embrace each other for a long time before Franklin pulls me away.

"Thank you," Dad whispers into my ear and I almost burst out crying.

Franklin leads me upstairs to the bridal suite. In the elevator, he takes my hand in his and shivers run up my spine.

"This is it," I whisper to myself.

I won't be able to push him away much further. I won't be able to say no anymore.

We have been engaged for months and we have barely exchanged more than a kiss or two. There was only one instance I remember when he put his tongue in my mouth.

I pushed him away for as long as I could but what about *tonight*?

"You were so beautiful walking down the aisle," Franklin says, intertwining his fingers with mine.

"Thank you." I give him a slight nod.

"I can't believe that we actually did this."

"Me either."

I glance up at him and our eyes meet just as the elevator reaches the top floor. It's a penthouse with an enormous bedroom, Jacuzzi tub, and floor-to-ceiling windows around every wall.

We are on the fiftieth floor so we're looking down at all of New York City.

It should be the happiest night of my life but I would rather spend tonight it in a roadside motel that charges by the hour than here with *him*.

"Would you like something to drink?" Franklin asks, walking over to the bar. I shake my head no.

"No, thanks, I've had a few glasses already."

"A few glasses? That's hardly any!"

I smile, knowing it's not my place to bring up how much he drinks even though I am his wife now.

I sit down and wait for him to pour a glass of whiskey and take a seat next to me. He drops his arm over my shoulder and pivots his body toward mine. I'm still wearing my wedding dress and I can hardly breathe.

"Thank you for today," he says.

"You're welcome."

I don't know how to respond before adding, "It has been a long day. I'm really tired."

"Well, why don't I help you get out of those clothes and you can put your feet up?"

He moves closer to me and I flinch. When he stands up and pulls me up to my feet, I take a step away from him. I want this to stop but I'm scared to say no. I have said no a lot and I have seen some aspects of his anger.

"I'll be right back," I say, pulling away from him.

In the walk-in closet, I peel off my dress and

drop it on the floor. I unbuckle the strapless bra digging into my rib cage and glide out of the Spanx holding in my stomach, finally letting out a deep sigh.

There is a fluffy, comfortable towel hanging by the bathroom, but I opt for the sweats that I packed in my bag.

When I come out, Franklin makes a sour expression on his face.

"Oh, no," he says, "I thought that you would bring your robe so we can be twins."

He's sitting on the edge of the bed with his legs spread out. His robe falls open just so I can see everything.

I freeze. I don't know what to do.

All the blood drains away from my fingers and I stare at him.

"Come here," he says, patting the bed next to him. "Come sit next to me."

I shake my head no.

"Come here," he says sternly.

When I do as he says, he turns to me and flashes a big wide smile.

Franklin tugs on my shirt and pulls me closer to him. I resist but only for a little bit. I can't resist anymore. I feel an obligation and for some reason I can't say no.

He turns my head up and touches my lips with his. Suddenly, I snap out of it.

"No. I can't!"

When I pull away, Franklin pulls me closer. He tries to kiss me again and I can't pull away.

"You're gonna say no on our wedding night?"

I shrug my shoulders.

"This is how you want to start out a marriage?"

"No. I don't, but the thing is that I'm not really feeling it. I mean, I know that we're married but what is this really? I mean, do you actually love me?"

"Yes, I do," he says, staring deep into my eyes.

"No, you don't. If you did, then we wouldn't be here. You wouldn't be making me do something that I desperately don't want to do."

I watch him breathe in and out, with great effort.

I watch him think.

I wait for him to try to kiss me again but he surprises me. Instead, he pulls away.

Without saying another word, he gets up, closes his robe, and walks out. He shuts the French doors behind him and turns on the television. I can hear the muffled sounds through the door.

I sit back down on the bed and wrap my arms around my knees.

"What are you doing?" I whisper.

These questions and about a hundred more swirl around in my mind until my head starts to pound. I go to the bathroom and fill a glass with water all the way to the rim and drink it without stopping. When it's empty, I fill it up again, only managing to drink about half.

I hadn't realized just how thirsty I was until this very moment. My headache seems to disperse a little and my thoughts become clearer.

Maybe he left me alone for now because he does actually care about me?

Maybe he's trying to be my friend?

Maybe he's trying to be a good husband?

I wash my face in the sink and search for the tube of moisturizer in my purse, I glance down at my phone instead.

Four missed calls.

They're all from Henry. There are also a number of messages. I stop myself from listening to the voice mail and from reading any of the messages.

My fingers itch to see what he has written.

I haven't talked to him since I was too much of a coward to tell him the truth of what happened at my father's house.

I left him a note and told him that I would love him forever and that part was true. I did all that to protect him and I thought that that would push him away.

Luckily, it hasn't.

Still, tonight, I don't allow myself to hear his voice or to read his words.

I stop myself, *not* because I don't want to hear it but because it feels like the right thing to do at the moment.

Franklin didn't force himself on me and I feel an allegiance toward him, no matter how slim.

Of course, how low are my standards that I am actually thankful that my husband didn't rape me? Be that as it may, I appreciate the gesture and I return it in kind.

AURORA

T he week after the wedding, we host a dinner party. Franklin has postponed our honeymoon to Bora Bora for a month or two, until all of the paperwork and negotiations with him taking over Tate Media are complete. Secretly, I'm relieved. I want him to be as busy as possible because then he might not notice me snooping around. If he's occupied, then maybe he'll be too tired to make a move on me at night.

I officially move into his palatial penthouse and though we are supposed to share the master bedroom, he allocates a room for me. It has its own en suite bathroom and courtyard as well as plenty of built-in bookshelves for all of my work.

I join the dinner party a little bit after the initial

few guests arrive but they are mostly Franklin's single male friends who work in startups. He introduces me to everyone and their names and professional titles come in one ear and go out the other.

I try to be pleasant and friendly but I take every opportunity to keep to myself. Luckily, the room is full of strangers who are only interested in congratulating me on our wedding and little else. They know that I'm not involved in the business of Tate Media and therefore I'm just window dressing.

I take my time ordering a drink and then slip out onto the balcony. I find a nook behind a large plant and hope that no one will spot me here.

Next time, I say to myself, I'm going to invite a friend or two to this thing. At least then I'll have someone pleasant to talk to.

A loud burst of laughter startles me and I press myself against the wall. The voices belong to a man and a woman but I don't recognize them.

"Are you sure that you're not cold?" the man asks. "You can have my jacket."

"No," the woman says. "I'm fine. I've had a little bit too much to drink so I'm good."

"I've never been here before," he says.

"I haven't either. I can't believe that I actually got an invitation."

"I know, right?"

"This place is insane," the guy says. "Have you ever been to an apartment this big?"

I start to feel very cold and debate whether I should just sneak out and go back inside but I have missed my chance. My only hope now is that they don't stay out here for much longer.

The voices get muffled for a moment but then they turn back toward the door.

I hear the woman ask, "So, do you think that's true?"

"What?"

"You know," she whispers, "the whole thing about Franklin being into young girls."

"I guess so," the guy says.

My mouth drops open. What is she talking about?

"Aren't you surprised?" she asks.

"I mean, we all knew that he was really into women, right?"

"Of course! Normally, I'd just say that Aurora is an idiot for marrying him if she thinks that he's not going to cheat on her but, come on, fifteen year olds? That's just not right."

"Wait, what?" he asks.

"You didn't know about that?" she asks.

"No! I thought that you were talking about him just sleeping around with, you know, women his own age or at least legal age."

"No, that is not what I heard."

As they go back-and-forth about whether or not this is true, my mind starts to race. I caught Franklin in bed with another woman but she was not underage. She was well into her twenties and she knew exactly what she was doing.

Could this be true? Could he really be coercing underage girls?

"How do you know about any of this?" the guy asks.

"Cynthia Lazaro told me. Her older sister worked as a maid for him last year at his property in the Hamptons. There were all sorts of rumors swirling around there."

"Why didn't she go to the cops?"

"You know why," the woman says. "She didn't want to lose her job. She was getting paid really well, a lot more than she ever got paid working at the Marriott and she had to clean a lot less."

The door to the balcony swings open, casting

light on my face. I inch further behind the bush to stay hidden.

"What are you two doing out here?" someone asks.

His voice is deeper, older, and clearly annoyed. "I'm paying you to work and circulate, not flirt. Get back inside!"

When the couple leaves, I let out a sigh of relief and rest my back against the wall. Did I really just hear all of that?

I walk back inside with a heavy heart. I need to find out the truth but how?

Of course I can't ask Franklin. He will just flat out deny it. This is yet another thing that I have to get to the bottom of and yet another thing that I have no idea how to tackle.

I head to the bar and refresh my tonic water with a slice of lemon, then make the rounds around the room. I walk briskly so that no one pulls me into a conversation. The few people that try, I wave to and promise to come back after using the bathroom.

Out of the corner of my eye, I spot Franklin near the library. Usually he is the one in the center of the room, holding court. This time he's leaning over a young woman in a waitress uniform of black slacks, a white button-down shirt, and a vest.

I watch him from afar, sliding my body just out of sight. He flirts with her and even touches her hair. Even if she's *not* underage, he has no shame. There are people everywhere. This is a party that we are hosting as a couple and yet here he is, making moves on someone else.

My purse starts to vibrate against my thigh. When I reach in and pull out my phone, I see that it's a call from Henry. I let it go to voice mail.

4

AURORA

I don't like to run. I don't like the way that my chest burns with each breath and I don't like how heavy my legs feel with each step. I can't run far without stopping. I have to take breaks when my air runs out and I get a pain in my side.

On this evening, at twilight, when the city is covered in a magical sheen, I force myself to put on my sneakers and run out the door. I can run on one of the machines downstairs but it's not the same thing.

Sometimes it's nice to take your mind elsewhere and watch a Netflix show or listen to an audiobook while pounding the rubber and setting the incline. Other times, it's absolutely necessary to get outside.

I need the fresh air.

I need the sound of the city.

I need to feel myself moving through space with each motion.

Franklin and I have still not had sex. The more I find out about him, the more certain I am that I don't want to be intimate with him, so if anything were to happen, it would be without my consent.

Honestly, I'm pleasantly surprised that he has not pushed the issue since the wedding night. He says that he's been busy, but maybe he is just occupied.

He has had lots of meetings with lawyers and various members of each department all in an effort to try to make this transition as smooth as possible. But given what I heard at the party, I wonder how much his lack of interest in me is a result of his keen interest in something else.

I pick up the pace and put one foot confidently in front of the other. The wind feels cold against my face. I pump my hands to get the blood rushing around but it does little to warm me up.

I walk past a mother rushing by me with a baby in a stroller as well as a golden retriever who is only too happy to be out and about. My mouth is parched and my lips are dry, cracked. My eye tingles and a tear forms, not from sadness but from a strong wisp of cold air that slices through it.

I want desperately to stop when I get to the first intersection but I force myself to jog in place, get a hold of my breathing, and keep going. When I pass a bodega and the smell of freshly baked bread consumes me, I am thankful for the fact that I never bring my wallet because I probably won't be able to say no.

The cramp in my side that started out as a little annoyance has ballooned into something that feels like a gut punch with each step. I don't make it to the end of the second block. I stop just short of the intersection, bending in half trying to get some air into my lungs.

I hate running. Did I ever mention that?

I walk for another block and start to feel better. My mind seems to become clearer and more focused. My thoughts are no longer jumbled together.

I still don't know what to do about Henry, Franklin, this marriage, or the Tate Media empire but at least I have the thought that I can come up with a plan.

I take my time going back home. I walk a lot and run in short little bursts but don't push myself like I did on my way out.

When I get back to my building, I get on the elevator and my mood shifts. Whatever clarity I just experienced, suddenly vanishes. Franklin's apartment is thousands of square feet and yet it's not enough.

Just as the elevator doors open, I see her. She has tears streaming down her face, which she wipes off with her sleeves.

"Hey, what's wrong?" I say as she tries to get past me and into the elevator.

"Nothing, nothing," she blurts out and continues to cry.

The girl looks to be around sixteen and that's being generous. She is skinny and barely 5'2. Dressed in jeans and a hoodie with her hair falling into her face, she looks like any teenager you would see on the street.

"What happened?" I ask her. "Please, you have to tell me."

"I don't have to tell you anything," she snaps and brushes my hand off her shoulder. "Let me go."

I hesitate to follow her down but I change my

mind at the last minute and put my hand out for the doors to open.

"What are you doing?" she asks, burying herself into the corner.

"What happened? Were you just with Franklin? Did he do something?"

"I have no idea what you're talking about," she says, hiding her head.

"Please," I beg. She hides within herself, clearly traumatized.

I try one more time.

"Please, tell me your name. You can trust me."

"You're his wife, right?" the girl asks, pulling her face slightly from behind her loose hoodie, just enough for me to see her.

Her eyes get wide just as mine narrow.

Suddenly, I recognize her.

"You were there at the party, right?" I ask. "I saw you two talking by the library."

"Get away from me," she says, swatting my hand away as I try to touch her.

She thinks that I'm upset about her sleeping with him, when it's something else entirely.

"How old are you?" I ask. "What happened? Please, you can trust me."

When the elevator doors swing open, she rushes past me and disappears down the hall.

When she glances back, I snap a photo of her.

5

AURORA

I ride the elevator back to the penthouse completely shaken up. I don't know what I'm supposed to do or what I'm not supposed to do.

There's usually an elevator operator here, pressing the buttons but today he's absent. Did Franklin arrange this, too, or is it just a coincidence?

I walk into the apartment and take off my running shoes in the hall closet. I walk quietly to the kitchen to grab a glass of water. After downing all of it, I stare out of the window at the New York skyline and wonder what the hell I'm supposed to do. If that girl was just having an affair with my husband, then that's one thing but if she was actually underage and if she was crying because he attacked her, then…

My thoughts trail off.

I knew that Franklin was a difficult and egomaniacal man.

What I did not know is the extent to which he could be cruel and unkind.

I walk to the far end of the apartment toward my bedroom. There are sounds coming from further away. My throat tightens up. It's still going on.

I walk to the back room, the master bedroom, and peek through the cracked door. The moaning is coming from them; Franklin is on top of her. I can't see her face, but it doesn't sound like she's protesting.

I clear my throat and he turns to look at me. I expect him to be surprised and to pull away but he doesn't. Instead, he winks at me and keeps going.

"Oh, no, who is that?" the woman asks, trying to get him to stop.

"Don't worry about her. That's just my wife," he says and thrusts into her.

This time I don't bother making a scene. I just go to my bedroom, close the door, and lock it.

I change out of my sweaty clothes and jump

into the shower, letting the hot scalding water rush over my naked body.

I stand here for a long time hoping that the heat will wash away some of what I've seen, but the visual is as strong as ever when I towel myself off.

An hour later, there's a knock on my door. I don't answer.

He knocks harder.

"Come on, Aurora, let me in."

"Go away," I say without looking up from my computer.

"Open the door. Now."

He knocks so loud that the door sounds like it's going to come off the hinges.

"I'm not kidding," he says and I force myself out of the bed.

I've been sitting in my best approximation to a yoga position and my legs have fallen asleep so it takes me a few steps to walk normally.

"I'm sorry you had to see that," he says.

"Me, too," I say through the crack in the door.

Franklin pushes it open and walks in. He sits down and pats the seat next to him. Instead, I pull the chair from the desk and position myself across from him.

"Come on, this is what you're going to be like?"

"I don't know what you want me to say," I say. "Do you want me to applaud you?"

"Listen, we already had this conversation. You made it perfectly clear that you didn't want to be touched and I have made it perfectly clear that until that happens, I'm gonna do what I wanna do."

"So, you'll stop cheating on me if I have sex with you?" I ask. "Is that what you're saying?"

"Well, you clearly have no interest in having sex with me. Why can't I be with someone else?"

I don't really have an answer to this.

What I really want to ask him is about the underage waitress who rushed out of our apartment with tears in her eyes.

What I really want to know is why did she look so scared?

What the hell did he do to frighten her?

But I keep my mouth shut. For now.

If I were to bring it up, he would probably deny it and that would be the end of it.

No, I need to find out more about her first.

"Listen, I don't know why you're getting so withdrawn," Franklin says. "I have tried to make a move on you. I have tried to take you out on a romantic date. I have tried to woo you, but you are rejecting all of my advances. I have needs and I have a lot of shit going on with this buyout so I need to let off some steam. I'm sure you can understand that."

"I feel like we've had this conversation already," I say. "Can you please leave?"

"Yes, we've talked about this a number of times but nothing is resolved. What do you want, Aurora? Do you want me to be faithful to you even though we don't have anything between us? What exactly am I going to be faithful to?"

I don't have an answer to that. The only thing I know is that I can't stand sitting across from him and him peering into my eyes.

I stand up, wrap my arms around my shoulders, and walk toward the window.

I stare at the skylight and wonder what all of those people below us are doing, thinking, and experiencing. Perhaps, if I try hard enough, I can transport myself to another world and not be here anymore.

Unfortunately, I'm not so lucky.

Franklin takes a few steps closer to me and touches my shoulder.

I flinch but he just pulls me closer to him. He pushes my hair off my neck and places his lips to my skin.

Shivers run down my spine but not the good kind. My heart starts to pound out of my chest and it's so loud that I can barely think.

I shake my head no and try to pull away from him but his grasp is firm and strong. "No," I whisper just as he puts his mouth over mine to shut me up.

"No," I say again, pulling away.

"Well, now, baby. Just let go. Trust me, I'll take you to the moon."

"No." I shove him away from me. "Don't you get that? I don't want you."

Instead of replying, he raises his hand and slaps me across the face.

I grab onto my burning cheek and glare at him.

"I'm so, so sorry," he says quickly under his breath.

He pulls me closer to him and apologizes over and over again. I shake my head trying to push him away but not so hard that he would slap me again. The violence came out of nowhere and the tenderness that followed confuses me.

"Aurora, I'm sorry. I have no idea what happened."

I don't respond.

"I just got so…angry," he continues. "But that

was way out of line. That was so fucked up. Please, please forgive me."

When I don't say anything, he continues to hold me as tight as possible.

His whole body is shaking as he repeats himself over and over again. It takes me a few moments to realize that the only way I can make him go away is to accept his apology.

"It's okay," I say quietly.

"Really?" he asks, giving me a kiss on the cheek.

I nod and he kisses me on the forehead.

"I just need to be alone now, okay?"

"No, you can't," he says. "You can't leave me like this. I feel like such an asshole."

Well, you are, I say silently to myself.

I force a smile and repeat my request. After a few moments, he finally caves.

"I have some work to do anyway," he says, walking out of the room. In the doorway, he stops and turns to face me. "But we're okay now, right?"

I nod, averting my eyes.

"Yes, sure," I whisper to get him to leave.

When the door closes and he disappears down the hallway, I pick up my phone and dial Henry's number.

6

HENRY

I haven't talked to her since the wedding. I've tried calling and texting but I haven't heard anything back. At first, I held a grudge. I was angry at her for not telling me what's going on and for leaving me hanging. I was angry with her for going through with the wedding. But then something occurred to me. Maybe Aurora only did it because she had no other choice.

That's when I decided that I would answer her calls *no matter what*. I wouldn't play the cat and mouse game. If she ever called, texted, or contacted me in any other way, I would be there. I would put away my pride and I would be *there* for her.

Why?

That's what people who love each other do.

Let's just say that it's easier to make this promise than to keep it. It has been weeks since I have heard from her after I had left her about a hundred voice mails and texts.

Then one night, one lonely Wednesday night, suddenly, I see her name on my screen.

A big gulp jumps into my throat.

My pride makes me want to reject her just like she had rejected me. I want to push her away. I want to make her wait. I want to tell her no she can't have access to me every time she wants it because she doesn't deserve that.

When the phone rings again, I press Accept.

"Aurora?" I ask.

"Henry, I'm sorry," she mumbles. Her voice is frantic and out of control.

"What happened? What did he do?"

"Nothing. Nothing happened."

"I don't believe you. Did he hurt you?"

"I'm fine," she says. I hear her take a deep breath and exhale slowly. "I'm sorry that I didn't call you earlier. I'm sorry that I left things the way that I did."

"Why did you?" I ask.

"I don't know," she says after a long pause. "I

was lost and I just got married and I thought that...
I don't know what I thought."

"What is going on? I thought that you were
going to go to your father and tell him that the
wedding was off."

"Yes, that's what I was going to do but then
something came up."

"What?"

"I can't talk about this now. Not over the phone.
Will you meet me?"

"I don't know," I say quietly. "I'm not in New York
City and I don't want to drive two hours just to hold
your hand when you have a fight with your husband."

That's a cold thing to say, but it's the truth. She
has to hear it.

"I'm sorry," she says. "Of course, I'm being
selfish. I just want you to know that I...*love* you and
that has never changed."

I shake my head, trying to figure out what to do.
I want to see her and I want to talk to her face-to-
face about everything that has happened but I don't
want to be the one making the first move.

"I really need to talk to you, Henry. It's not
about us, it's about everything that is going on. I
need your help."

I let out a sigh.

"I'm going to be in the city tomorrow. I'm working in the office now, two days a week. We can meet for lunch."

"I'd love that," she says as her voice cracks.

I SEE Franklin at work during our weekly meeting. I would be lying if I said that I didn't feel a pang of guilt over meeting up with his wife. The only reason why I'm here, working in this high-rise is because of him.

He gave me a chance when no one else did and he even wrote me a very generous check to cover all of my mother's pancreatic cancer procedures.

The insurance was useless when it came to experimental treatments and barely covered the chemotherapy and radiation as it was. Thanks to his thirty-thousand dollars, I was able to prevent her house from going into foreclosure, stay on top of all of the medical bills, and hire a nurse to take care of her when I couldn't be there.

I suggest that we go to a restaurant but Aurora said that we should meet in the lobby of a three-star hotel that caters to business travelers. I don't know why I'm here but I grab a seat in the lobby near the window and answer some emails on my phone, waiting for her to arrive.

Aurora walks in dressed in jeans and a form-fitting blue sweater that accentuates her graceful body. She tosses her hair nervously from side to side and it bounces as if she were a model in a shampoo commercial.

I don't think I have ever seen anyone as beautiful as she is right now. She sits down next to me without giving me a hug or even touching my hand. When I reach out to her, she pulls away. She looks around cautiously and whispers, "I can't."

"How are you?" I ask.

"I'm okay," she says quietly.

She's lying but it's too early for me to press her. For a second, I just want to stay in the moment. I just want to lose myself in everything that is *right* between us, rather than dwell on all of the things that are wrong.

Aurora stares into the distance, somewhere behind me, and I look at her face in her hands for signs of pain.

Did he hurt her?

Did he force himself on her?

Has she had sex with him willingly?

I don't know the answers to any of these questions and I will not find them out here.

"I need to talk to you," she says after a moment. "I got a room. Number 513. I'm going to go upstairs now. You stay here and follow me up in five to ten minutes. Please make sure that no one is following you. We cannot be seen together."

She gets up before I can nod. She heads to the elevator and disappears behind the stainless doors.

I glance at the television screen in the lobby and stare at the gray-haired anchor talking about the fires in Australia. When a sufficient amount of time has passed, I go upstairs.

7

HENRY

I knock on the door of her hotel room and as soon as I walk in, Aurora closes it, nestling herself against my body. She holds me tightly and begins to sob into my shoulder.

"I have missed you so much," she whispers over and over again.

I drape my arms around her and hold her tightly as wave after wave of tears flows through her. I rub her head slightly, bury my hands in her hair promising that everything will be okay. I make this promise over and over again knowing full well that it may be a lie.

"What happened?" I ask when she finally pulls away from me. "Did he hurt you?"

She shakes her head but refuses to make eye contact.

"What did he do?" I make a tight fist, bracing myself for impact.

I should have fought for her. I should've stopped the wedding.

Have I just stood by as this monster attacked her?

"He… He didn't really do anything," Aurora says quietly.

She walks away from me and sits down on the edge of the bed. Burying her fingers into the comforter, she finally looks up at me. Her lipstick is smeared and there are track marks of mascara rounding the apple of her cheeks.

"Tell me everything," I insist. "Don't leave anything out."

"Only if you promise to not hurt him," she says after a long pause.

This time both of my hands fold into fists. She glances down and sees the whites of my knuckles. Shaking her head, she glances up at me.

"No," she says sternly. "Absolutely not."

"What?" I ask, forcing my fingers to relax.

"You're not going to attack him," she says.

"I can't make any promises. Tell me what happened."

"I won't tell you a thing until you make me a promise. I need your help and fighting is not going to solve this problem. It's gonna make you feel better but it's not going to get to the bottom of every terrible thing that is going on."

She's right, of course, she's right. I take a deep breath and sit down. I turn toward her and take her hand in mine.

"Okay," I say with resignation in my voice. "I promise I won't do anything but please, tell me what happened."

———

As AURORA GOES into her story, I let out a small sigh of relief when I learn that Franklin didn't force himself on her. But then she mentions that he had slapped her and rage boils up within me.

"I can handle Franklin," she says calmly. "At least for now. He doesn't seem that interested in me, which is a good thing."

"Okay," I say slowly, unsure as to where she is headed with this.

"I need your help with something else. I saw this girl running out of our apartment. She was crying and really distressed. I saw Franklin talking to her at the party we hosted. I tried to get her to tell me what happened but she was too afraid to say a word. Maybe she thought that I would get upset because I'm his wife. Who knows?"

Aurora pulls out her cell phone and scrolls through her photos.

"I took this picture of her," she says, showing me the screen. "Just as she was leaving but luckily, I got a little bit of her face. I don't know if it's enough but is there any way that one of your investigators could find out who she really is? Maybe even talk to her? She's not in trouble. I'm just worried that…"

"What?" I push her.

"I heard something at the party," she says quietly.

The expression on her face turns from upset to serious.

"I heard these two people talking about how Franklin is into underage girls. This girl," she says, pointing to the screen, "she didn't look very old and I don't know what happened but I suspect that whatever he did, it wasn't consensual."

"Holy shit," I whisper.

"Yeah, holy fucking shit."

We sit quietly for a while as I try to process what she has just said. I knew that Franklin was fucked up but that's *really* fucked up.

Suddenly, Aurora starts to cry again. I take her in my arms and she buries her face in my chest.

"I just feel so guilty," she mumbles in between sobs.

"Why? What did you do?"

She shakes her head and refuses to answer. Her whole body begins to shake. When she calms down for a little bit, I raise her head up to mine and look deep into her eyes.

"You did nothing wrong," I say, wiping her tears.

"I just keep thinking that maybe this is my fault."

"What are you talking about?"

"Maybe if I just let him have me. Maybe if I hadn't resisted him and… maybe he wouldn't be doing *this*."

"No, you're wrong. If he's into little girls, then there's nothing that you could've given him to change that."

It makes me sick to my stomach to even think about this.

Aurora doesn't believe me. She shakes her head, averting her eyes.

"He would do this regardless," I say. "You have to believe me. If he's into that, then no matter what you would have done it wouldn't have been enough."

She gives me a slight nod and buries her face in my shoulder. I pull her close to me and kiss the top of her head. When she looks up at me, I kiss her cheek.

Suddenly, something has changed. This moment of tenderness morphs into something else. I look down at her luscious lips and watch them part slightly.

I glance up into her eyes to make sure that it's okay. She gives me a slight nod and I press my lips onto hers. Our mouths open and everything outside becomes a blur.

I run my fingers over her neck and down her spine. I hear her exhale quietly as we kiss.

"Is this okay?" I whisper.

"Yes," she mumbles.

I kiss her harder. Our tongues find each other's and she presses her body against mine. I feel the softness of her breasts and the intensity of her grasp as she buries her fingers in my hair.

But then she pulls away.

"No," she says, shaking her head.

"What's wrong?" I ask.

"I don't know but it feels wrong. I'm married."

That statement pushes all the air out of my lungs. It feels as if I have been punched in the gut.

"I'm sorry," she says, draping her arm around me. "I know that this is so…complicated."

"No," I say. "It's not complicated. It's stupid."

She narrows her eyes and stares at me. I glare back.

"You're not married. I mean, perhaps you're married on paper but we both know that it means nothing. He's forcing you to do this to get what he wants and you're going along with it to get what you want."

Aurora doesn't respond. Instead, she pulls her hands away from me and places them on her lap.

"You don't have to be so cruel," she says.

"You don't have a real marriage and you know it," I continue. "I'm here for you. I want to help you. I don't want to pretend like we don't have anything between us. Those sparks that you feel in the pit of your stomach are not something you can deny."

She doesn't say anything. I'm tempted to go on but I force myself to stop. She has been through a lot and another fight is the last thing she needs.

But I'm angry.

I'm fuming. Just not at her.

I'm pissed at Franklin for making her feel like she is doing something wrong.

I get up and walk over to the window. There isn't much to look at but the building across the street and the parking lot below. Looking up, I search for the sun through a blanket of low-hanging clouds.

"I will help you get to the bottom of this," I say with my back toward her. "You don't have to worry about that."

"I'm not," she says and I suddenly realize that she is standing right behind me.

She puts her arms around my waist and squeezes me tightly.

"I shouldn't have said that," Aurora whispers.

"It's okay, it doesn't matter."

"No, it does. I love you, Henry. You were the person that I was thinking of when I was walking down the aisle."

I turn around to face her and furrow my brows.

"What are you talking about?" I ask.

"When I picked out my wedding dress, I imagined that I would be wearing it to marry *you*. When I walked down the aisle, I transported myself to another world, one where we could be together. My wedding night? I wished more than anything that it was with you."

I pull her closer to me to give her a hug but she puts her hand on my chest and looks up instead. Standing up on her tiptoes, she presses her lips to mine.

Our tongues find each other's and I lose myself in her. She presses her fingers into my back as I bury my hands in her hair.

She tilts her head back and I run my lips down her neck and bury my face in her bosom.

Her breasts move up and down with each breath as I cradle them in my hands. Her fingers make their way toward my stomach, pausing briefly at my belt buckle but not letting it stand in her way.

After undoing it, she pulls out my shirt and unbuttons it. I flex my stomach and watch her eyes light up at my protruding six-pack.

She runs her fingers slowly over each muscle,

licking her lips in anticipation. I like the way that she looks at me.

What I like more is looking at her.

I lead her to the bed and push her down. I climb on top of her and she pulls me closer. Our lips touch again as she helps me out of my shirt.

I slide my hand underneath hers and push my way up past the lace covering her breasts. She lifts herself up a little so that I can unclasp her bra and I don't wait for her to take it off before I take her into my mouth. Her nipples are hard and aroused and her moans make my dick as hard as a rock.

When I make my way to the other one, my phone goes off.

"Just ignore it," I say but her body stops moving.

I glance up and see that she is looking at the screen.

"It's your mom," she says, swallowing hard.

"What time is it?" I ask, searching for the alarm clock near the nightstand.

"Shit," I say, pulling up and answering the phone. "I'm sorry I'm running a little late, I'll be there as soon as I can."

"I'm so, so sorry," I say, shaking my head. "I

completely forgot that she had an appointment in the city today and I said that I'd be there with her."

I button my shirt and pull up my pants.

"It's okay," Aurora says, adjusting her bra.

We kiss again but she pulls away and tells me to hurry.

"Send me the picture of that girl," I say when I open the door. "I'll try to find out who she is."

I can't get Aurora out of my head for two days. Every time that I close my eyes, I kiss her and I run my fingers up and down her soft skin and I lose myself in her luscious lips.

This afternoon is no different. I'm back home in Montauk and my mother is having a really good day. She's alert and up and about, with newfound energy. Kathryn Solinski, the nurse, has been going far and beyond her normal duties by doing the cleaning, the laundry, and even some grocery shopping.

When my mom was first diagnosed with pancreatic cancer and she was buried under all of those bills, she entered a dark period. It's as if there was a cloud hanging over her, infecting every thought and action but with Kathryn's help, and her companionship, she finally started to have something to look forward to. She started to enjoy the little things in life and I saw how much of a difference that has made.

I haven't told her much about what's going on with Aurora but she knows that I miss her. She also knows that she's married.

While my mother was enthusiastic about me trying to get back together with her prior to her marriage, she has been less so afterward. She doesn't say much but she never asks about her and I can tell that she silently disagrees with the fact that I still see Aurora.

Jackie, my old friend and an ex-police officer who now makes his living spying on married people to gather evidence for their divorces, comes over. My mother is in such high spirits that she actually makes us dinner.

"You really don't have to, Mrs. Asher. Henry and I can just grab something from the fridge or get take-out later."

"Nonsense, I finally have a guest over and I am feeling great. I'm not going to pass up this opportunity to act like a hostess."

Jackie glances at me waiting for me to say something but I just shrug my shoulders. When my mother gets something in her head, it's hard to convince her otherwise.

"So how are you feeling? Any news?"

"Actually, I'm feeling good. I'm not as tired as I used to be. The chemotherapy is definitely taking a toll but I'm sort of used to it. I have to go get more tests done and then I will know more about whether it has spread."

"Well, you've been amazing through this experience," Jackie says. "I'm really sorry that you're going through all this and I hope that it all turns out well."

She gives him a slight nod. We all know that the survival rate of pancreatic cancer patients is not the best, but hope is all I have and hope is all I can hold onto. I take a sip of water before my emotions get the better of me.

My mom hasn't seen me cry once and for that I'm grateful. She has enough problems and she's being strong enough for me that I can't break down in front of her.

I'm here to be her rock. I'm here to support her and to do anything that she needs me to do for her.

When my mom and Kathryn disappear into the

sitting room for some coffee and biscuits, Jackie and I clean up the dishes. We don't have a dishwasher so I wash as he dries and puts them away.

"I got that image that you sent me," Jackie says.

"And?"

"I did a reverse image search on it and it's not good." He pauses for dramatic effect. I wait, annoyed.

"Well, are you going to tell me?"

"She's still in high school."

My mouth drops open.

"How can you be so sure?"

"I found her pictures on Facebook from a few years ago when she was in middle school. Then I found her Instagram. She's definitely in high school. Tenth grade."

"Holy shit," I whisper and shut off the water. I help him dry the rest of the silverware and put on another pot of coffee.

"What now?" I ask.

"I have no idea."

"But Aurora told me that she saw her working as a waitress at their party. She couldn't have had that job if she was still in high school, right?"

"There's more," Jackie says, stirring some sugar into his cup.

I watch the cream dissolve in the blackness at the bottom of his coffee cup and wait for him to continue. This time he's not pausing to create drama but simply gathering his strength.

"I reached out to one of her friends. There was a photo where a girl commented saying that she will always be there for her no matter what. It made it seem like she knew something or something may have happened. The dates lined up so I direct messaged her. I told her that I was a private investigator and I used to be a police officer and that she had nothing to worry about but I needed to talk to her about something very important. We video chatted and I recorded our conversation.

"Do you want to see it?"

I nod and hold my breath as he opens the recording on his phone.

The girl who appears on the screen doesn't look like she is a day over fourteen. She's skinny and small and her eyes look terrified.

Luckily, she is wise enough to ask Jackie for his identification and even ask for his private investigator license number, refusing to continue the conversation until she looks it up online. After she confirms his identity, she relaxes a little bit and lets out a sigh of relief. She says that she's not comfortable meeting but she will tell him what she knows.

"Tell me everything," Jackie says from behind the camera.

The girl adjusts herself in her seat, avoiding eye contact and looking out somewhere in the distance.

Finally, she takes a deep breath and says, "Taylor would kill me for telling you any of this but I think someone has to so that it doesn't happen again."

"What happened to her?" Jackie asks.

"There's this really popular girl in school, Tamara, who always has really expensive shoes and jewelry and purses. One day, Taylor was talking to her in study hall and she told her that she does these massages for this guy who lives in this mansion. She made it sound like all she does is go to his house and gives him a massage. I thought that it could never be just that but Taylor is really innocent and a little bit stupid."

She takes a deep breath.

"Tamara said that he just likes looking at high school girls and having them massage him and he would pay them $200 per hour for doing this. No sex, no anything."

"So, that's what she did?" Jackie asks.

"Yeah. Tamara told her that she first had to go to the house and work as a waitress but she would get paid for that also. That would pay $100 an hour plus whatever tips anyone gave her. That was the first level. If she got past that, then she would be invited back to do a massage."

"What happened then?"

"Then Tamara gave her the address and told her about everything that was going to happen and how it had absolutely no sex and how he wouldn't even touch her. She really needed the money. She would never have done this otherwise. Her parents are going through a divorce and her stepdad is really abusive and he's threatening to take her little brother away and her mom can't afford a lawyer. That's why she did this. It wasn't to get a fancy purse or anything like that."

"Of course not," Jackie says. "Even if she did just want a purse, it would not make what Franklin did any less wrong."

"I know," the girl says. "I'm just trying to explain that Taylor is not like that."

"What happened then?" Jackie asks.

"I don't know most of the details because she

wouldn't stop crying but apparently, he was lying naked on the massage table and he told her to get naked. He wouldn't take no for an answer and at one point he even yelled at her. That's when she got really scared and took off her clothes. He touched her. He told her to go down on him and then she massaged him. After that, he touched himself and she had to watch."

Anger starts to boil up within me. I stare at my fist ready to punch something or someone.

"After he handed her the money," the girl continues, "he gave her an extra hundred dollars, and she was so distraught that she freaked out when she ran into his wife in the elevator. His wife kept asking her what was going on but Taylor was freaking out because she didn't want her to think that they were having an affair."

"That's pretty much it," Jackie says, turning off his phone.

"She cried for a while after that and I told her that everything will be okay and that I will do everything in my power to help her friend," Jackie says.

"Holy shit," I say.

"Yep."

"He's a rapist and a pedophile," I add.

"Yeah, I know," Jackie says, staring into space.

"What're we gonna do about him?" I ask.

"We have to stop him."

9

AURORA

I meet up with Henry three days later and those are the longest three days of my life. Every hour away from him is excruciating. I crave him and I need him.

I want to touch him more than anything I've ever wanted in the world. I'm waiting for him on my father's boat. He knows the address because this is where we had first met.

I leave it open and sit downstairs in a form fitting black dress. It's cold outside so I wore my trench coat here so that I could show off my legs. The heels are uncomfortable. I don't bother with the Spanx because I want to be comfortable and I know that he loves my curves.

The boat is slowly heating up, but it's still cold

enough to see your breath inside. I'm grateful for the long sleeves and the scarf. While I wait, I play a game on my phone and check social media but mostly I think about Henry.

The last time that we were together, we came very close to actually making love. He had an appointment set up with his mom's doctor and he had to rush off but I hope that tonight we can make up for what we didn't have the opportunity to finish.

Whatever guilt I used to feel about Franklin and my so-called marriage, has disappeared. I made him a promise but it's not a promise if someone is practically holding a gun to your father's head. But it's even worse than that. Franklin doesn't care about me as his wife. If he did, then he wouldn't have strange women in and out of his bed almost every day.

I crack my knuckles to try to make the anger that's bubbling up within me go away. This is supposed to be a good night. I won't let my so-called husband ruin it.

There's a knock on the door and I tell him to come in. Henry comes downstairs dressed in a slim pair of jeans and a formfitting jacket that hugs every muscle in his chest. I get up and practically run into his arms.

When I imagined this moment in my head, I saw myself sitting seductively on the couch and crossing one leg over the other. I saw myself kissing him softly and passionately and holding his hand tightly as I led him to the bedroom.

Now, seeing him in the doorway, I can barely stop myself from charging at him. It's silly and immature yet it's exactly how I feel and I'm so happy that he opens his arms and welcomes me inside.

We have both waited so long for this moment.

We can't wait any longer.

When I rush him, I jump into his arms. Henry carries me to the bedroom. I laugh and kiss him over and over again. Our kisses are sloppy and out-of-control. My hair falls on top of his face and everything between us intermingles.

Henry plops me onto the bed and I bounce. He stands before me and I reach up to unbuckle his jeans. I push them down to his ankles along with his boxer briefs. His ass is round and his thighs are the most massive and muscular ones I've seen. He flexes them as I look for a moment admiring the strength that I see before me.

I laugh and then I shift my eyes to his hard dick. It's large and hard and I can't help but reach over and wrap my fingers tightly around the base. I bring my lips to him and open my mouth. As he slides inside of me, Henry leans his head back and moans.

He is so big that he fills up my whole mouth and my jaw feels like it's going to lock with each move. After a few moments, I pull away and run my tongue up to his belly button and then stand up to kiss him. Our mouths touch and our tongues intertwine. This time, there's nothing tender about our kiss. We have been there and we have done that. Tonight, we want it dirty, quick, and delicious.

He flips me over onto my stomach and pushes me down onto the bed. I love the way that he handles my body, directing me in every move. It allows me to let go and to enjoy the moment, the way that I normally can't.

I hear the crackling of a condom wrapper somewhere behind me but before I can even turn around, Henry drapes himself over me, pressing himself into my back.

I can't help but arch and pull myself off the bed just a little bit. His hands find their way into my dress and over my breasts. Then he turns my head to the side and moves my hair off my neck. As he slides inside of me, he starts to run his tongue over my neck and up to my ear.

"I love you," he whispers with each thrust.

I whisper something back but it all comes out muffled.

"I love you," he says. "Don't you ever forget that."

"Do you hear me?" Henry asks, pushing into me again and again.

"I hear you," I mumble. "I love you, too."

Henry's movements become faster and faster and I can't handle it any longer. I try to hold it off as much as possible but suddenly, the pressure that has built up in me explodes, and I let go. Waves of pleasure rush through me as his thrusts move faster and faster.

My whole body shakes as he pushes me more and more into the bed.

"Aurora," he says with a huff, repeating my name over and over again. Lying in each other's arms afterward, we exhale simultaneously and nuzzle together. Nothing has ever felt so right.

"I love you," Henry whispers.

"I love you, too," I say, kissing him softly on the forehead.

"I love you more," he says louder and with more confidence.

I laugh.

We gaze into each other's eyes and I find his lips with mine.

10

HENRY

"That was amazing," she says. "I forgot how sexy you are."

"You did?" I ask, propping myself up on my elbow and scrutinizing her face.

"No, that's not what I meant."

"I hope not."

"I just meant that I forgot how good we are together and how good you are at this."

"You're not so bad yourself," I say, smiling at the corner of my lips.

We lie here for a long time, just enjoying each other's company. I listen to the steadiness of her heartbeat and the quietness of her breaths. She plays with my hair, twirling a strand around her index finger over and over again.

I want to stay in this moment forever but I can't. It's fleeting and in a few more minutes, she'll have to get up and go back to her normal life.

"I want to think of this as our wedding night," she says quietly.

I squeeze her gently and kiss her neck.

"It can be," I say.

"No, it can't. I'm already married."

"It's not like your marriage is consummated," I point out.

"Lucky for me, I guess," she says.

I see the pain in her eyes and I will do anything to make it go away.

"Don't go back to him," I say. "Let's just run away together."

"Where would we go?"

"California? Hawaii? Alaska? Paris? Buenos Aires? Anywhere you want."

"Tell me about it," she says. "I want to see what our life would be like."

"We will get a small apartment, right in the middle of the city. I will get up early and buy you some freshly baked scones and piping hot coffee. We will eat breakfast in bed and stay in our pajamas all day. In the afternoon, we will take a stroll around the city, I'll buy you fresh flowers and we'll go to the farmers market. On weekends, we will do picnics in the country or by the beach."

"That sounds marvelous."

I look at her as she loses herself for a long time in this other life that we could have. I've never been to Rome but I have seen plenty of postcards and movies and I imagine myself walking down those cobblestone streets holding the hand of the woman I love.

"Where do you want to go?" I ask. "I'll take you anywhere."

"I wanna go everywhere," she says. "Just not now. I can't leave him alone to do what it is that he's doing. I can't let him ruin Tate Media. I can't let him kill my father. I have to stay here and fight for what's mine and you do, too."

I give her a slight nod, disappointed.

"Your mother needs you. We can't leave right now. She has to get better and you have to be there for her."

She lets out a deep sigh and shakes her head.

"In that case, let me tell you about what Jackie found out," I say.

I haven't brought this up earlier out of fear of

ruining the mood. She was waiting for me and she wanted me and I wanted her and I didn't want anything to stand in our way. But now, I have to tell her the truth.

"Franklin is a lot more dangerous than we thought," I say slowly.

She gives me a nod and signals for me to keep going.

Jackie had sent me the video that he recorded and instead of telling her what is on it, I just hit play. Aurora shakes her head as she watches, burying her head in her hands. She glances up at me a few times, her lips quivering.

"I can't believe this," she says over and over again.

"What do we do now?" she asks after I turn it off.

"We need more proof," I say with a heavy heart.

I don't want to put her in anymore danger than she already is but we need to gather more evidence. It's not that no one will believe the girl, it's that Franklin is a very powerful man and it will take a lot more than us to bring him down.

"I don't want to tell you to do this," I say quietly. "This is the last thing I want."

"What?" she asks.

"I worry about you and I don't even want you staying in the same house as him but if you want this to come out and if you want him out of Tate Media, you'll have to set up some recording equipment and try to catch him in the act."

11

AURORA

I don't know how to process what I've seen on that video. The girl was so small and the story that she was telling was so big and frightening that it just consumed my whole life.

Franklin is not a good person but I didn't realize that he was evil. I didn't realize that he was capable of such devastation. The girl cried for her friend and I cried along with her. On top of that, I felt incredibly guilty for practically attacking her in the elevator and forcing her to talk to me. Naturally, she was horrified when I tried to make her talk to me. She was traumatized and I just made it worse.

The guilt and regret consumes me as I meet up with Henry at another nondescript hotel room.

When I knock on the door, Henry opens it and gives me a warm hug along with a kiss on the lips. Out of the corner of my eye, I see someone sitting on the couch and quickly push Henry away.

"What's wrong?"

With my heart pounding out of my chest, I nod in the guy's direction.

"It's okay, that's Jackie. He's a PI. You can trust him."

I hesitate but step from one foot to another. The fewer people that know about this the better off I'll be.

Jackie comes over and shakes my hand.

"You really have nothing to worry about," he says.

Still, it would be better if you didn't see us kissing, I say to myself.

"Henry and I have been friends for a long time and his secrets are safe with me."

I give them a slight nod, feeling a little bit of relief.

"So, what am I doing here?" I ask.

Henry leads me to the table at the far end of the hotel room and points to all of the equipment that they have laid out.

"Jackie brought all of this today and he's going to show you how to use it."

I glance at the camera, the wires, and the lenses, shaking my head.

I thought that I'd be able to do this but now I'm not so sure. It's not the technology that's scaring me, it's something else entirely. Whatever Franklin is doing is very wrong and he knows it.

What would happen if he were to catch me?

"I know this is really scary," Jackie says, "but this is going to be the only way that you can find out the truth about your husband."

I already know the truth in my gut, I want to say.

"It's possible that nothing has happened," Jackie says. "There's a chance of that."

"No, there isn't," I say.

Jackie shrugs.

"You weren't there to see that girl's face. I rode down in the elevator with her. She was traumatized. He did something terrible in there and we all know it."

I say these words as much for his benefit as my own.

There are all these thoughts in the back of my

mind that have the possibility to stop me from believing the truth but the more that I can say stuff like this out loud, the stronger I become.

I'm afraid you can't be courageous if you're not afraid.

I take a deep breath and let him show me all of the technology and how it works.

After Jackie goes over it a few times, I connect all of the parts together myself a few times just to make sure that I know exactly what to do. He watches and nods approvingly. When we're done, I see Henry sitting on the edge of the bed with his head bent down.

"What's wrong?" I ask.

"I just really wish that you didn't have to do that," he says.

"Me, too," I agree.

"Maybe we can just go to the police? Maybe they can interview Taylor and Tamara and even Franklin and who knows what will happen."

"You know perfectly well what they'll say," I say.

He shakes his head. I sit down next to him and put my arm around his shoulder.

"I don't want you to do this."

"Of course not," I say. "If we go to the police now, that girl is not going to tell them the truth.

Even if she does, he's going to lie. He's going to lie through his teeth and he's going to get every lawyer out there to lie for him. He's going to stonewall this thing just like all of those other assholes and he's gonna put so much garbage out there into the media that no one will believe her. Then he'll come after me."

Henry glances up at me.

I give him a nod.

"You know that I'm right. He'll blame me. He'll know that this somehow came out because of me and he'll be right. No, before we go to the police, we need proof. We need a lot of evidence so that this whole thing can be completely irrefutable."

"I'm just really worried about you," he says quietly.

I squeeze his hand.

"I know you are but I'm going to be all right," I say.

"I want to believe that, but how can I?"

"I can only do my best. I'm going to set everything up and you're going to have all of the recordings so that if anything were to happen…"

"Don't you dare think like that," Henry says, pointing his finger in my face. "I will not let anything happen to you. He will not find these cameras."

"I know, I'm just saying in case…"

"There is no in case," he says with rage in his eyes. "He will not hurt you. I will not let him."

12

AURORA

I told Franklin that I was just going out on a short run, so unfortunately, I can't stay here long. As soon as I pack up the cameras and all of the equipment into my bag, it's time for me to leave.

"Are you sure that you can't stay longer?" Henry asks, holding onto my hand. "We can order some Indian food and have dinner."

"I'd love to but I have to get back. Franklin's working late today and I want to be able to set all this up before he comes home."

"I understand," he says with sadness in his eyes. He walks me to the door but I stop him from escorting me all the way downstairs.

"The fewer people that know about our relationship the better and that includes the hotel staff," I say.

When I touch the door handle to open it, he kisses me. He buries his hands in my hair and presses his lips hard against mine. My mouth opens and I let him inside. The fire that exists between us does not fade. In fact, with his lips on mine, it starts to rage somewhere deep inside my core. If only Jackie wasn't here, the…

"Listen, I can give you some privacy. I have some work to do anyway," Jackie says.

There's a hopeful expression on Henry's face but I shake my head no.

"I'm sorry but I really have to get back."

FRANKLIN ISN'T HOME when I get there and I let out a sigh of relief. I look at the clock. He said he would be late but this is quite late. I debate as to whether I should try to put something together now or just wait until tomorrow. I decide to do one room.

I set up the tiny camera just as Jackie had shown me and hide it behind the oversized plant in his office. I keep checking the time on my phone while I listen for anything in the hallway and make a quick decision to do the same thing in the master bedroom. The girl on the recording mentioned that Taylor was in his office. I had caught him with another girl in the bedroom. These are probably the main rooms where he would do something like this.

Before I get a chance to put up anything to block the camera, I hear the front door.

My heart sinks.

Shit, what the hell do I do now?

I hear his footsteps coming down the hallway and it's too late to take down the camera. I quickly move the picture frames from one side of the dresser to another and pray that he doesn't notice.

"Hey," I say, hopping onto the bed and pretending like I had been there the whole time.

"What are you doing here?" Franklin asks, looking tired and disheveled.

"Just lying down," I say, shrugging my shoulders. "I'm not feeling very well."

He walks over to me and sits down on the edge. He slumps his shoulders and when he looks at me, his eyes look weary.

My whole body tenses up. I force myself to relax. My phone is lying next to me and when I reach for it, he grabs it out of my hand.

"Are you seeing him?" he asks.

I freeze, not knowing what to say.

"Are you seeing Henry?" he asks again. This time his voice is more urgent, annoyed.

"I don't know why it matters," I say. "You've been seeing *everyone*."

"That has nothing to do with anything. I'm not sneaking around sleeping with my ex-boyfriend."

"I thought that's what we had," I lie. "You made it perfectly clear that you wanted an open marriage."

"I did no such thing," he says, furrowing his brow. "We never talked about anything like that." His voice is loud and intense. If he's trying to intimidate me, it's working.

I reach for my phone but he closes his hand around it and pushes me away.

There's a lock and he doesn't know the password.

He turns toward me and glares. "Are you going to unlock this or not?"

I try to remember whether I have any

incriminating evidence on the phone. I mean, there are messages between Henry and me but are there any messages about Franklin and what he did to that girl?

I don't think so but I can't be sure.

Shit, I have been so reckless.

"I need the code," he insists.

I shake my head no.

He leans over to me, so close that when he opens his mouth, I can smell his breath.

"Tell me the code," he says and a little drop of spit lands on my cheek.

I again shake my head no.

He doesn't ask again.

Instead, he grabs my hand and forces my thumb onto the fingerprint recognition circle. I wince from the pain.

He doesn't let me go until the phone unlocks.

I rub my hand tenderly trying to make the throbbing go away. He doesn't apologize and I swallow hard, waiting for what's to come.

He is in my messages. My heart starts to beat so hard it's practically jumping out of my chest. I take quick shallow breaths to try to calm down but it's all to no avail.

"You're seeing him again," he says quietly.

"We're friends," I whisper. "I thought you wanted us to be friends."

"No," he says sternly. "You're not friends. You're lying."

I let out a slight sigh of relief, realizing that I was lucky enough not to discuss anything too personal over text. All that Franklin suspects is that I am cheating on him. That's not great but it could be a lot worse.

"Are you seeing him?" he asks.

I shake my head no.

"I don't believe you," he says.

"Why do you care anyway? I've caught you sleeping around with… how many women is it?"

"That doesn't matter. I'm a man."

"Exactly, you're just like me."

"No, I'm not," he says, shaking his finger in my face. "I can do whatever the fuck I want and you can't."

I don't know how to make it stop or how to make him go away. I don't want to make it worse but I have to stand up for myself.

"Henry is just a friend. Like I said before," I say it as calmly as possible.

"You don't text like this to a friend." He shows me the screen.

I stare at the words "I love you" and pray for them to give me strength.

"That was just him texting me when he wanted us to get back together. He's going through a lot with his mother and he is my ex. As you know, the breakup has been hard and—"

"You're a fucking bitch!" He punches me.

It comes out of nowhere. I've never been hit before and the pain catches me by surprise.

The hurt is localized to my eye but it quickly spreads in waves. I can't see anything as my vision goes dark.

Another blow sends me to the floor and something that tastes like iron gushes into my mouth. I grab onto my nose trying to contain the blood and the pain gets worse.

Tears stream down my face but when I open my mouth, nothing comes out. My cries are lost somewhere in the back of my throat.

The third jab hits me right in the stomach. I topple over in half and stay there, covering my head with my hands.

"Don't you ever sneak around behind my back again," Franklin hisses into my ear.

Out of the corner of my eye and through the tears and the pain, I see him lift up his fist again. I close my eyes and brace myself for impact but nothing comes. Instead, Franklin just tosses my phone on the bed next to me.

"You don't get to do whatever the fuck you want," he says. "You're my wife and I own you."

13

AURORA

Alone in the room, writhing around, I let out a sigh of relief. The throbbing doesn't stop, but it's not just the physical pain that hurts me.

I knew that Franklin Parks was capable of a lot of things but I had no idea that he was capable of this. I never thought he would raise his hand to me. Not like this.

That was naïve. When he slapped me across the face in anger, perhaps then I should have run away but I didn't. I stayed put but things only got worse.

I should have known the person that he was the minute that he laid his finger on me. In another world, I would have never said yes to this wedding and this marriage.

It's almost as if everything that I have known has gone out of the window. I'm lost and with every passing moment, I go deeper and deeper into the abyss.

My nose is throbbing and when I touch it, I recoil from the pain. Still, I can't help but bring my fingers close to it again and try to feel for something. I force myself off the bed and drag myself to the bathroom.

The reflection in the mirror makes me sick to my stomach. My eyes are swollen shut and my face is covered in blood. My nose is still bleeding and the skin around it is puffy and turning blue.

I have never seen anything like this before, except in a movie. My father is capable of a lot of things but he had never laid his hands on my mother, me, or anyone else that I know of. I try to figure out what to do.

Do I put ice on this?

Do I wash off my face first?

Should I go to the hospital?

I take a washcloth and put it under the stream of hot water. I dab it lightly and press it to my face. Even the slightest pressure is hard to bear.

My thoughts return to Henry. If Franklin's

capable of doing something like this to *me*, what is he capable of doing to *him*?

And then something else occurs to me.

Did he actually think that I was having an affair or is this just a ploy to get me to confess to what is really going on?

These questions along with about a hundred others speed through my mind but I can't come up with any answers. The person that I thought Franklin was had somehow disappeared. I didn't know much about him but I was certain that the things that I knew were right. Then suddenly, I discovered things that made him someone else.

I would have been a lot more careful with my phone calls and texts if I had any idea that it actually bothered him. He had been so nonchalant about his own affairs that I thought that he existed on a whole other plane of existence.

He wanted to marry me even though he knew that I didn't love him. He wanted me as a trophy and we both knew that. He invited Henry over for dinner and acted like we could all be friends but not once did I ever suspect him having even a tinge of jealousy. Then this happened.

"What the hell?" I ask myself out loud, staring

into my eyes in the mirror. "What the hell just happened?"

Despite how I look now, there are some things that I should be grateful for. Luckily, he did not discover the cameras. He doesn't know that I had planted them but I have not had a chance to see if all of the connections are right.

I return to my phone and tap over to the secret folder in the back. The app looks just like a regular news app on the outside. That's on purpose.

I click on it and hold my breath. I had set everything up just as Jackie had showed me but I was supposed to make sure to double check that it broadcasts to my phone before I left. Franklin had come in before I could do that.

I tap my fingers on the counter before forcing my eyes onto the screen.

"Oh my God," I whisper, just under my breath. "There it is. The image of the master bedroom along with his office are crystal clear."

I click on the back of the file, the previous recording, and watch him punch me over and over again.

It's an out of body experience. This just happened to me and here I am watching it as if it is happening to someone else. I want to pull away but I can't.

The door swings open and I close the app with one quick motion and click on Facebook.

"How are you feeling?" Franklin asks.

"Okay, I guess," I say, turning toward him.

I brace myself for impact but by the way that he is standing in the doorway, I can tell that he's here for something else.

"I just wanted to…check up on you," he says quietly. "I didn't want you to be hurt."

I want to say, *Well, then you shouldn't have attacked me,* but I bite my tongue.

"Maybe I should go to the hospital," I say.

"No, absolutely not."

I touch the washcloth on my face and try to wipe away some of the blood, wincing in pain.

"Here, let me do this," he says. I sit down on the toilet and let him wash the blood off.

He is surprisingly gentle, not pressing too hard when the pain gets too much.

"I don't think that your nose is broken," he says. "Just badly bruised."

"Well, that's something, I guess," I say, shaking my head.

"Listen, I know that this was really fucked up and… I just want to apologize."

"Okay," I say slowly, elongating the second part of the word.

Does he really think that an apology is enough?

On the other hand, it's a lot more than I had expected so, perhaps that's something.

"You can't go to the hospital but I'll call a nurse to come in and check up on you."

"A nurse?" I ask.

"Yeah. She's a private medical professional who makes house calls for people who want to keep things away from prying eyes."

That's one way of putting it, I laugh silently to myself.

My phone rings and we both glance down at the screen. When I see that it's Henry, my blood runs cold.

"Answer it," Franklin instructs.

14

HENRY

I don't have a reason to call her but I do anyway. I miss her and I need to hear her voice. I also want to know if she has set up the recording equipment and if there's anything else to worry about, but mainly I want to know that she's okay.

"Hey there," I say. "How are you?"

"Fine. How are you?"

She pauses for a moment in between the word fine and the question.

"What's going on?" I ask.

"Nothing, just hanging out."

It sounds like something is off. It's almost as if someone is hovering over her but I can't quite tell.

"Do you want to FaceTime?"

"No," Aurora says very quickly. "I mean, I can't right now."

"So, I wanted to ask you about–"

"Yeah! I would like to arrange something for the two of you again," she says, interrupting me.

I furrow my brows and glance down at the phone, making sure that I have heard her right.

What is she talking about? I wonder but I don't ask.

"Chelsea was asking about you and I think that Franklin and I can put something together again, if you want."

"Yeah, I'd like that," I lie.

My heart starts to beat very fast. I clench my fists and stare down at the whites of my knuckles. We never talked about Chelsea.

She's telling me this because something is wrong. Franklin is there. He's either listening or we're being recorded. She's telling me this for a reason.

"I guess I can call Franklin and talk to him about that but I wanted to just touch base and… well, you know how I am. I'm not the bravest around hot girls."

She lets out a nervous laugh. "No, of course not. You don't have any moves at all."

We continue to banter back-and-forth but my mind begins to race. How could I have been so stupid? Why weren't we more careful with meeting up or talking on the phone? What *exactly* does Franklin know?

"Listen, I have to go. I'm running late for Pilates."

My heart sinks. Aurora doesn't do Pilates.

"Listen—" I start to say something but she cuts me off.

"I really have to go," she says and hangs up.

In a fit of rage, I throw the phone across the room and onto the bed.

No, no, no! This isn't fucking happening. She promised me that everything would be all right but she can't make a promise like that. I make a fist and punch the pillow on my bed but it's too soft and it doesn't make enough of an impact.

I throw some jabs at the bed. It's firmer and I imagine that it's Franklin's face that my hand is colliding with. With each punch, my rage multiplies and I let out a primal yelp.

When I open my eyes, I come face-to-face with the wall and it takes all the strength of my body to not drive my knuckles through it.

No, I take a deep breath and exhale slowly. I'm

going to save my hand for when I drive it into his nose.

THE FOLLOWING MORNING, I go into work unsure as to what to expect. I brace myself for the worst but I promise myself that I will not betray Aurora and attack Franklin outright. That's not going to accomplish anything.

If this is a game that we have to play, then I'm going to not only play but also win.

I work in the office a few days a week and this is my usual day. I get in early, check my emails, and jot down some notes from the last interview that I conducted.

I don't have the same freedom working here as I did when I traveled to the Midwest but I appreciate the opportunity and the job. It keeps me close to home and I still get to do the podcast.

Nowadays, the format has shifted a little since I can't do that many interviews. Instead of investigating the story myself, I simply rehash and go over a number of famous crimes from the past. Currently, I'm working on the O.J. Simpson case.

People my age and decades older remember the

trial and all of the news coverage leading up to it but the younger generation doesn't know many of the details. It's my job to inform them.

Surprisingly, this new format is going well and attracting new listeners every day. Say what you will about Franklin but he has an eye and an understanding for what the market wants.

The other thing that I really appreciate about this job is how much less work it entails. Investigative reporting is not only a full-time job but one that often requires eighty-hour work weeks. It involves a lot of tracking down leads and going after people, requesting interviews over and over again until they finally agree.

With this new approach? All I have to do is review the stories and articles that have already been published, synthesize the story, write out the script and make it sound interesting.

My office phone goes off and it's Carolyn, the personal assistant for the floor and all of the reporters here.

"Mr. Parks would like to see you in his office," she says in her usual cheery voice. She's the only one who has ever asked about my mother's treatment and I really appreciate her concern.

"Thanks, tell him I'll be up in a little bit."

"No, he wants to see you now. Says it's urgent."

My blood runs cold. I clear my throat and say, "Sure, I'll be right up."

When I hang up the phone, I exhale slowly.

What do you want? I wonder. Did you catch Aurora with the recording equipment? Is everything over? If so, why do you want to see me in your office?

15

HENRY

When I get to his office, I see Franklin on the phone, facing away from me. He sits in his impressive, royal blue satin wingback chair and waves to me to come over. I take a few steps forward and don't close the door until he turns around and points at it.

"Listen, I need this done or you're getting fired," Franklin says and hangs up.

He looks at me and says, "Honestly, some people just can't be bothered to do any work without a threat."

"I didn't realize that you were such a hard boss," I say, smiling at the corner of my mouth.

Franklin tilts his head and brushes his fingers through his hair.

"Well, you just happen to be very good at your job, otherwise you'd find out just how difficult I can be to deal with."

The calmness in his voice sends shivers down my arms. If he suspects that something is going on and is acting like this, then he is a much better actor than I have ever suspected him to be.

"Don't just stand there," he says, offering me a seat. "Do you want something to drink? Coffee? Tea? It's probably too early for a martini, right?"

"Well, it is just after eleven."

"The day that I've been having, I could use a stiff drink but I think I'll hold off until noon otherwise I might not make it through the rest of the day."

"What's going on?" I ask.

"You don't wanna know. The merger is really taking a toll on me and I'm tempted to just say fuck it."

"Why don't you? I'm sure that will make your wife happy," I joke.

He looks up at me, narrowing his eyes and then he starts to laugh.

"I'm not so sure," he says, tilting his head. "Well, I don't know what Aurora is thinking but her father won't be happy."

I nod, not exactly sure where to go from here.

"So, how's everything? How's your mom feeling?"

"She's doing well. Chemo and radiation are hard but she's keeping her spirits up. Thank you again for everything that you've done," I say. "That money has been invaluable."

"Oh, shit, don't even worry about it," he says, waving his hand. "I was just asking about her health but I'm glad to hear that things are good."

"Well, they're good under the circumstances. She has to go in for some more tests and that's always a scary time. There's a lot of waiting and seeing."

"Ha! Isn't that the thing about life?" Franklin asks. "Seems like we're all just waiting around to die, aren't we?"

I'm taken aback by his statement and I straighten my shoulders, squaring off with him.

"No, I'm sorry," he says quickly. "Crap, that was a really fucked up thing to say."

"Don't worry about it."

"See, that's exactly why I need a drink. Nothing I'm doing or saying today seems to be any good."

"Don't worry about it," I repeat myself after a long pause.

"So, Aurora tells me that you want us to set up another date with Chelsea," Franklin says, changing the subject.

"Yeah, I'd like that. Is that okay?"

"Of course! More than okay. I'm glad to hear it. When I saw that you and Aurora had been talking so much, I sort of got something else in my head about you two."

My breath gets stuck in the back of my throat but I don't make a move.

"What are you talking about?" I ask as nonchalantly as possible.

"Well, you know, I grabbed her phone instead of mine one day and I saw all the messages that you guys have been exchanging, so…I got a little worried."

"Really?" I ask, totally surprised. "Why?"

He shrugs. "You are her ex…"

"Wait, you didn't actually think that we were spending time together… romantically?"

"Yeah, a little bit," Franklin says, leaning slightly toward me. He's analyzing me, challenging me but I'm not going to reveal what I think.

"Hey, you were the one that wanted us to be friends, remember?" I point out. "I was perfectly fine not ever seeing her again but you insisted."

"I know, I'm such an asshole. I was the one that invited you to our house and set you up on that date."

"Speaking of which, that's actually the kind of girl that I'm interested in. Chelsea. Hot, rich, single. What more does a single guy in the city want?" I ask.

"Perhaps an ex-girlfriend who has recently married a billionaire?" Franklin asks.

I stare at him and he glares back. Neither of us blink.

"I'm just kidding," he says after a moment, starting to laugh.

I join in and our roar fills the room.

"Well, I'm glad to hear it," Franklin adds. "Otherwise, I would probably be a little bit more concerned and a lot less accommodating."

I sit back in the chair, not sure how to interpret his sudden change of mood.

"So, you don't want me to talk to her anymore?" I ask.

"No, of course not. I'm not an asshole."

I wait for him to continue but he doesn't. Instead he reaches over, picks up a pen off his desk, pressing the top in and out a few times while I wait.

"So, how's everything going with the podcast? Any problems?"

"No, not really. I'm just busy going through all of the articles and I've been watching everything that they ever put out on O.J. Simpson. It's kind of a big job."

"Yeah. That was the biggest story in 1994 and he kept selling newspapers and driving ratings throughout the 90s."

"Yeah, I remember seeing it on TV," I say. "It was always the top story. That's why I think the listeners are so interested in it. There's a whole new generation of people that only vaguely came in contact with it when they were kids."

We talk about it for a while and the various angles I should pursue to give the podcast a fresh feel. He has some good suggestions. I listen and take notes.

"The thing about O.J. Simpson is that I am a married guy who can understand where the hell he was coming from," Franklin says as our conversation starts to wind down.

I scowl at him.

"What do you mean?" I ask.

"He was a powerful guy with a really hot wife and she was fucking someone else."

"Are you saying that it's okay that he did it?"

"No, not exactly." He waves his hand. "Although I have to admit, I see where the man was coming from."

"But he was doing the same thing. He was cheating on her with almost every other woman in town, possibly even her best friend."

"So?" he asks. "Does that give her permission to cheat on *him*?"

"Yes, why not?" I ask.

"Nope," Franklin says, shaking his head. "Don't believe that shit that women are putting out there. Men and women are different and that's a good thing."

Flabbergasted by his misogyny, I don't know how to respond.

"C'mon now, don't look so shocked. Remember, we're men. We take what we want and we want the impossible."

16

AURORA

The following day, Franklin calls me from the office and tells me that he wants to have dinner with me. A formal dinner. He wants me to dress up and put on my makeup, do my hair, go all out, and he wants to have a date. I'm not entirely healed, not even close but I don't think he wants to see my bruises, so I do my best to camouflage them.

Franklin called me a nurse and she came over. She even offered me Vicodin. I turned her down and said that I would deal with the pain myself with a little bit of Advil for good measure.

I wish that I could go to the hospital or the police and make an actual report about what happened but it is too risky. I need to get him on my side. I need to find out more about him and about his involvement with my father and Tate Media before I make this case. If he thought that hurting me would put me in my place, he was wrong. It just made me angrier and more determined.

At least, that's what I keep telling myself as I get ready for dinner.

It takes me a long time to put on the dress and zip up the back. My ribs throb with each breath and I don't have much range of motion in my arms.

I put on a pair of high-heeled boots and cover my shoulders with a cloak. The black cocktail dress is a familiar one, my go-to item whenever I have to dress up.

I don't know if it's just me but I don't like to wear fancy things. Sometimes, the thing that scares me the most about going to certain places and dealing with uncertain situations is wearing unfamiliar clothing. That's why I chose this one for this occasion. I have been inside of it and I know what it's like.

Just like on my wedding day, my hair, my makeup, and my dress will be my armor. It worked then. I just hope that this is enough to protect me now.

When I come downstairs, my heels make a loud clicking sound on the marble.

Franklin is standing in a three-piece suit in front of a roaring fireplace with a glass of whiskey in his hand. He's tall, slim, and wide-shouldered.

He is beautiful on the outside but incredibly cold on the inside. He is what romance novels are made of but our relationship is nothing like that. Some people can be changed. He's not one of them.

He's evil incarnate and he's damned. The only little thing left to do is to bury him underground and never put up a gravestone.

When I walk up to him, he turns around and pulls me in. He kisses me lightly on the cheek. Instead of pushing him away, I turn my other cheek toward him, presenting it for a kiss.

Franklin touches his lips to mine but only slightly, not pushing me to return the gesture. I don't.

I take a step back, cold and collected. I am here but if he wants me to be here in a good mood, he will have to do a lot more than that.

"I know that you're still angry with me," he says, "So, let's have some food first."

I follow him to the formal dining room where

dinner is almost served. I sit next to him at the table that spans the entire wall. For a second, I'm tempted to take the seat at the far end but this is a safe place to talk and I want to take advantage.

The waiters serve wine and appetizers. I take a piece of bread from the bowl and bite into its delicious softness. I've been trying to avoid carbohydrates but tonight I need all the strength that I can muster.

We talk about the weather and his workout at the gym and nothing else in particular. I don't watch much Netflix or television and he doesn't read many books so we don't even have popular entertainment in common.

"I know that I should probably not bring this up," he says, putting his fork down. "It feels like an elephant in the room."

"What does?" I ask.

"All of that stuff that happened," Franklin says without batting an eye.

"I'm not sure how I'm supposed to respond to that," I say after a long pause. I put a strawberry from my salad into my mouth and taste its explosive flavor.

"I just want you to know that I'm sorry."

"You said the same thing when you smacked me," I point out.

I know that I'm pushing my luck but I hope that we can have a real conversation here, not something topical and without substance.

"I know," he says with a long face. "Sometimes, I just get so full of rage that I lose control of who I am. It's hard to explain."

"I don't know what you want me to do."

"I want you to forgive me."

"Okay, I forgive you."

"No." He shakes his head. "You're lying."

"I don't know if I can forgive you, just like that. I mean, you're sorry now but what if it happens again?"

"It's not going to," he promises. "I'm sorry. I'm such an asshole."

"Yes, you are," I say. "But I guess you're my asshole."

He looks up at me and gives me a smile.

"You mean that?" he asks.

I shrug and look up at him after a moment.

"Please don't ever do that again," I say.

"I won't, I promise." He reaches over and grabs my hand.

He squeezes it tightly and a shiver of fear rushes

through me. This is a different side of him but right around the corner, I know that a darker version is lurking.

I thought that I knew what would make him snap. I thought that I could control the monster but now I know that he can come out from anywhere, at any time, and the only thing I can do is steady myself. For now, I'm just grateful that he seems to be at peace. We have made amends and that's good enough.

17

AURORA

Later that evening, Franklin takes a call from work and disappears in the middle of dessert. I'm relieved. After happily finishing my tiramisu, I take a second slice to my room. There, I get out of my heels and into my sweats.

Just as I get into bed and settled in with a cup of tea and something mindless on my tablet, my phone goes off. I see that the camera that I had set up had started recording. I quickly turn off the notification so it never goes off in the future and wait.

I turn my attention back to Netflix but my curiosity gets the best of me. What is going on in *there*?

The camera is set up as a motion detector so it

only records when someone is in the room. I click to the secret folder and, when the screen loads, my mouth drops open.

I see Franklin standing in his office, wearing nothing but a robe. There's a girl whose face is away from the camera. She is small, diminutive even, and dressed in jeans and a tank top. Her hair is in pigtails. Instead of waiting for her to leave and getting onto the massage table with a towel over his butt, the way that it's customary to do in legitimate spas, he just drops the robe and watches her.

I feel sick to my stomach. Physically ill, I rush over to the bathroom and dry heave but nothing comes out. After a moment, I glance at the phone again. Now, he's lying down on his stomach on the massage table.

I don't want to watch. I want to make it stop.

If I drop this phone and go over there right now and interrupt them, it will come to a stop. She won't get hurt but I also won't have much to show anyone. It will just be my statement against his and that's if the girl sides with me. If she doesn't, then I'll have nothing.

I don't know what to do. I don't want to be complicit in this. I want to *help* her. I don't know what's to come but I see the wreck coming. The train is coming around the bend, it has already derailed and it's about to crash right into her. I have to stop it but I can't make my body move.

I'm terrified. Franklin has already done a terrible thing to me and that was *before* he knew that I knew his secret.

What else is he capable of?

I don't know how much time passes. I debate with myself over and over again about what I should and shouldn't do. Minutes continue to tick away.

When I finally force myself to look, the girl is crying. Her head is hanging low and her shoulders are moving up and down with each sob. Franklin pulls away from her and I realize that he had made her go down on him.

I shake my head in disbelief. Tears stream down my face.

I didn't stop this. I was here and I was too afraid.

I hate myself and I hate my cowardice.

Franklin says something but I can't make out what it is. The girl continues to cry, this time turning toward the camera. That's when I realize who she is. She's the one who I ran into in the elevator.

She came back!

"Why did you come back? Don't you know that he's a monster?" I whisper at the screen.

More tears come and my body starts to shake as much as hers. When she doesn't respond to whatever Franklin is saying, he spins her back around and points a finger in her face. He looks angry. Pissed off. Just like he did when he hurt me.

That's when I realize that she came back for the same reason that I didn't help her. We're paralyzed with fear and when the paralysis is strong enough, you will do anything just to survive.

Suddenly, the door opens and someone else comes into the room. He's tall, wide-shouldered, and older than Franklin. He's dressed in a suit and has an expensive haircut. He looks familiar but I can't place him. Then, I remember. He is the governor of New Jersey.

I'VE ONLY SEEN him on the news. He is middle-aged, balding, and rather round. He laughs and says something to Franklin, completely ignoring the girl in front of them. I shake my head as more tears start to well up. I know what he's about to do. I can't let it happen, no matter the consequences.

I rush over to the door and grab the handle but when I turn it, it doesn't open. I try again and again.

"What the fuck?" I stare at the door.

It's locked.

My mouth drops open. Franklin actually locked me in here. He knew this was going to happen and he didn't want me walking in on them.

I try the door again and again but it refuses to give.

I even try to break it down but the mahogany is too strong.

I pace around the room trying to figure out my next move. I'm still holding the phone in my palm but I don't dare look at it. I know that it is recording and there's nothing that I can do to stop whatever is happening. The only thing that I can do is not watch it.

A few minutes pass and then a few more. I crack my knuckles. I sit down on the bed and get back up. I walk from one side of the room to the other like a caged tiger. I don't know how to make any of this stop. Eventually, the curiosity gets the better of me and I look down at the screen.

There are now two other girls in the room. Franklin and the governor surround them. They touch all of them. I look at the girls' faces but I don't recognize them. They don't look much older than the first one.

The familiar nauseous feeling starts to build in the pit of my stomach.

Franklin laughs and then takes a step back from everyone else. I see the smile on his face as he turns to face the wall and looks almost straight at the camera.

My heart sinks and I hold my breath.

"No, no, no," I say over and over again. "Please don't see me."

I look closer trying to figure out if he is just looking at the picture behind which I hid the tiny lens or if he's looking directly at me, knowing full well that I am locked in here and watching him.

His gaze goes up along with his arm and I see him mess with something that looks a lot like my camera in the corner of the room. The only problem is that it is not *my* camera.

When he returns to the girls, I stare at my phone trying to figure out a way to rewind. I don't know if it will stop recording if I start clicking around so I let it go.

Did I just see him do that? I ask myself. Is he recording this?

I don't know why he would want to have a recording of himself doing any of this but I can think of a few reasons for why he would want to have a recording of the most powerful man in New Jersey frolicking around with some underage girls.

That's the kind of thing that can give you a lot of leeway when you need a favor or two.

When I pace around the room this time, my thoughts are more focused. If he's recording himself with them, who else does he have recordings of?

I now know exactly why everyone is so afraid and accommodating with my husband.

Now, the only thing to do is to find the videos.

18

AURORA

When I discover that Franklin is recording not only himself but other men with those underage girls, I search my room for any cameras and recording equipment.

Luckily, Jackie has shown me what the really small and really good ones look like and where to hide them so I know what to look for.

First, I check the lamps. Then the headboard. I go through every nook and cranny of the room and then check it all again just to make sure that I didn't miss a thing.

I go to bed with a heavy heart and I sleep restlessly. My sleep is so light that I hear him come to my room in the middle of the night and unlock the door. The lock moves very quietly and it would be easy to miss if I wasn't already on high alert.

I let out a sigh of relief. So far, he doesn't know that I know. I'm only safe for as long as that continues.

The following morning, when Franklin is gone and the housekeeping staff isn't around, I begin the search for the videos. I look through all of the cabinets in his office. I rifle through the desk and the bookcases. There are papers, bills, pens and pencils, and manila folders, but there are no memory sticks.

I search for close to two hours, looking through everything and then carefully put everything back. If a folder or an envelope was sticking out halfway, then that's how it goes back.

LATER THAT AFTERNOON, I meet up with Henry and Jackie.

This time, I don't dare go to a hotel room. We meet in public, at a coffee shop around the corner from Henry and Franklin's building. If someone is following me, then our meeting will look like an accident.

After I order something to drink, I slip my phone into Henry's hand and he disappears into the bathroom. A few minutes later, after transferring the files, he walks out with a blank expression on his face.

I watch him get in line and order some food while occasionally glancing over at Jackie who watches the video on Henry's phone.

We sit for a few minutes without saying a word. I guess I'm supposed to start but I don't know what to say.

"So, that was Governor Barbour?" Jackie asks, taking a sip of his coffee.

I nod, staring into space.

"Holy fuck," Jackie says.

"Did you have any idea he was doing that?" Henry asks.

I snap my head and glare at him. "Of course not. I had no idea he was recording anyone or that anyone else was even involved."

I nod and add, "There's something else."

They look up at me. I break off a piece of a blueberry muffin and shove it in my mouth. The flavor is explosive and it makes me feel better but only for a moment.

"He's recording them," I say.

"What?" Henry asks.

"If you look closely, you'll see it. I thought that he had spotted my camera and that it was all over but then he moved away and adjusted his."

"Why would he do that?" Jackie asks. "Why would he wanna incriminate himself?"

"He's probably going to cut himself out," I say, sitting back in the chair and tapping my fingers on the table. "He's doing it for evidence, power. If he has a recording of the governor doing this, then he can get him to do anything and to stop anything from coming out."

The three of us sit here and process this realization.

"I spent the day looking for his recordings. I thought that maybe there's a thumb drive or some sort of external hard drive that he kept in the house but I couldn't find a thing."

"What does that mean?" Henry asks.

I glance at Jackie and wait for him to explain.

"He must store all the files on his computer."

"It's what I think," I say. "He always has his

laptop with him and it's password-protected. I don't know the password."

"It must also be thumbprint protected," Jackie says. "That's a good thing."

"How's that?" I ask. "I can't very well use his hand to open his laptop without him knowing."

"Actually, you can."

A small smile forms at the corner of his lips, giving me hope.

"You need to find me something that Franklin has touched with his thumb; a used cup or something like that. Something that he held. Then I can make a dummy thumbprint that you can use to get into his laptop."

I nod, trying to think of what I can find.

"He drinks his coffee from an insulated mug," I suggest.

"It can't be anything that he will miss," Jackie insists. "You don't wanna be caught with that."

"Sometimes he uses plastic water bottles when he works out," I say.

"Yes, that's perfect," he says. "If he tosses it, then he's not going to miss it."

After we agree on a plan, Jackie leaves to go on another job. Not wanting to spend too much time with Henry alone in public, I tell him that I have to get back.

"I want to see you again," he says.

I shake my head and whisper, "No, he's on to me. It's too dangerous."

I walk out of the coffee shop and head down the street, taking a shortcut to the park through an alley. Henry catches up to me. I look around to make sure that we are all alone.

"What happened when I called you?" he asks. "Something was off."

"Franklin is really unpredictable," I say with a heavy sigh.

I don't want to tell him what happened. I know that I will only make things worse.

"Did he hurt you?" Henry asks.

I shake my head no, hoping that he doesn't look at my face too closely. I'm wearing about a pound of makeup and after watching a couple hours of YouTube videos, I have gotten pretty good at camouflaging the bruises. The problem is that they are still there.

I walk away from him but he follows me.

"You can't do this," I say, turning around. "If he sees us together, he's going to make me pay."

"What do you mean? What did he do?"

Out of the corner of my eye I see him make a fist.

"You can't do that," I say, pointing my finger up in space. "You saw the video. You saw what he's capable of. We have to take him down but we need to expose him. Everyone in the world needs to know the truth and that's the only way that it's going to work. You punching him in the face is not going to do anyone any good. Least of all me."

His nostrils flare but I can see that my words make sense.

Henry straightens out his hands, stretching his fingers, and then cracks his knuckles.

"I know," he starts quietly. "I'm not going to do anything to fuck this up. You can trust me."

"Good," I say, letting out a sigh of relief.

Henry looks around and then pulls me closer to him. He touches his lips with mine and all the pain that I have felt seems to vanish but then when he pushes me against the wall, I wince.

"What's wrong?" Henry asks. "Are you okay?"

I swallow hard, trying to gather my breath.

"I barely touched you," he whispers.

I give him a nod and raise my hand to wave him away.

"Everything's fine," I say after a moment.

"No, it's not," he says, tugging on my shirt. I try to push him away but it's too late. He lifts it up and gasps. When I try to pull it down, Henry follows it up around and sees the bruises up and down my back.

"What the hell is going on?" he asks.

I don't answer.

"Did he do this?" he roars.

I shake my head no and tears start to flow down my cheeks.

"Did he do this?" Henry roars again.

I am crying too much now to stop. As I wipe my face over and over again with the back and the front of my hand, I suddenly realize that I am removing my camouflage. Henry paces back-and-forth and when he comes back and looks directly at me, his eyes become two saucers.

"Your face," he whispers and touches me gently.

I turn away from him, averting my eyes. He pulls up on my chin and briefly touches my cheeks.

I can't see what he's looking at but I know what's there. The bruises underneath the foundation peek through. He's careful not to rub too hard but my secret is out.

Suddenly, Henry lets out a primal yelp. It's filled

with a kind of rage and anger that I have never heard before.

He makes a fist with his right hand and drives it into the palm of his left. If there was a wall around, he'd probably push it right through it.

I gather my thoughts and get a hold of my emotions. I wipe away the last of my tears and stand before him without a single lie between us.

"This doesn't change a thing," I say. "We still need to do what we need to do and you can't go in there and attack him."

He paces back-and-forth, letting out a few grunts of discontent.

"I'm sorry that I lied but I just didn't want you to feel like you're feeling right now."

"Oh, and how's that?" he asks.

"Helpless," I whisper, putting my hand on his shoulder. He brushes me off and turns around.

"You know that I have to get that print for Jackie and get that laptop. Who knows how many other girls and women he has done this to? Who knows how many other powerful men he has recordings of? They all have to go down. We have to bring them all to justice otherwise… he'll just keep doing it."

"Franklin deserves to pay for this," Henry says, his words barely audible.

"He will. He hurt me but not in the way that he has hurt all of those women."

Henry looks up at me, narrowing his eyes.

"He punched me and he physically assaulted me but he hasn't forced me to do anything sexual."

"Not yet," Henry says. "If you go back there, what is going to stop him?"

"I don't know," I say after a long pause. "For some reason, so far, he is taking no for an answer."

When I try to touch him again, he brushes me off.

"I'm the one that he hit and you are acting like this is all about you," I say.

"It's not," Henry admits. "I know. You're right. I'm just so… angry."

"Me, too, but you have to channel that anger somewhere else. You have to give me time. You can't make this worse otherwise they will all get away with it."

He gives me a slight nod.

"You need to promise me, Henry. Promise me you won't betray me. Promise me that Franklin will not know that anything is off until I get that laptop and we get a plan together."

"But what if something happens to you in the meantime?"

"I don't know," I say, shaking my head. "That's just a gamble that we have to take. If I don't do this, then no one will ever find out and I can't live with that."

We stand here looking at each other for a long time. Finally, he gives me a slight nod.

"Okay," he says. "I promise."

19

AURORA

When I get home, Franklin is already there. He's waiting for me right by the front door. My hands start to shake but I bury them in my pockets. I force a smile on my face and pretend that nothing is going on.

"Where have you been?" he asks.

"Just out, had some coffee."

"Is that so?" he asks.

I give him a slight nod, take off my jacket, and hang it in the closet.

He's standing a foot away from me, waiting. He doesn't move so I have to physically walk around him.

His moods are getting the better of me. I never know what I'm about to come into.

"Are you okay?" I ask.

"Yeah, perfect. Just wondering where the hell my wife is and what she's doing with her days."

"I was just out. I thought that you were at work. How's everything going?" I ask, trying to change the subject.

"Fine," he says. "We should be signing all the paperwork in a couple of days and Tate Media will officially have a parent company. What do you think about that?"

"I know that it will make my father happy," I say.

"What about you?"

"Honestly, I don't know if this would've been my decision. I prefer autonomy, but my father insists that this is the best thing."

I'm dancing around what I really mean, a bit clumsily.

"You're a very difficult woman to please," Franklin says.

"No, I don't think so."

"Well, you're married to me and you don't seem happy."

"You don't seem to be particularly happy to be married to me either," I point out.

"Why would I be? You don't want to touch me with a ten-foot pole and we are newlyweds."

"Is that what this is about?" I ask. "I already told you. I walked in on you having sex with, what was it, two young women? It doesn't make me feel very cozy or positive about our relationship."

"I wouldn't have done that if you were at all accommodating."

I shake my head.

"You don't agree?"

"I don't wanna talk about this anymore. I feel like all we do is go in circles."

"Okay, then," Franklin takes a step away from me, "what do you want to talk about?"

I want to say, *how about the fact that you locked me in my room while you attacked two teenage girls*, but I don't.

"Have you seen Henry today?" Franklin asks and my blood runs cold.

I'm not sure how to answer. A part of me wants to lie but we were right around the corner from his building, on purpose. I met in a public place because I didn't want it to look like I'm sneaking around.

"Yeah, actually. I ran into him and Jackie, his PI, at Starbucks down the street."

"Oh, yeah?" Franklin asks.

I give him a nod and say, "Yeah."

He looks at me for a few moments, moving his jaw from one side to the other. If he's trying to intimidate me, it's working.

"I thought that I told you not to talk to him again."

"I just ran into him," I say. "Nothing is going on."

"I want us to be an open book."

"Me, too." I nod.

"I don't want to worry about you being with your ex."

"Then don't," I say. "I'm not."

I'm tempted to bring up one of his affairs, but I bite my tongue. He can have as many consensual sexual relationships as he wants with women his own age. I don't give a fuck. In fact, I wish that he would find someone that he'd want to be with so that she can take my place.

"I don't wanna fight with you anymore, Aurora. This conversation is getting a little boring," he says, pointing his finger in my face.

His voice is quiet and low but he's not agitated.

I want it to stay that way.

"I don't wanna fight with you either," I say. "I don't want you to think that there's anything going on because there isn't. I'm married to you and Henry is nothing but a faint memory."

"I like the sound of that," he says, pulling me closer to him.

My heart skips a beat but I don't push away. Not yet.

He's just being friendly. I don't want to assume anything that would make this worse.

Franklin gives me a kiss on the cheek and I turn my head and put it on his shoulder.

Accepting his tenderness, I don't want to push him away but I don't want to turn it into something else either.

He holds me for a while and I let him. I listen to the beating of his heart as my own continues to skip beats.

His breathing is slow and deliberate. I listen to him inhale and exhale. I feel my body move along with his with each breath.

"This is nice," Franklin says. "Isn't it?"

"Yes, it is."

Of course, it's not. He's holding me captive. There's not a physical barrier separating us but rather one of fear. If he were anyone else, I would push him away and tell him to leave me the fuck alone but I can't.

He's my husband. I need him to think that he's my friend at least for the time being. He doesn't know that I'm playing a game that I can only win if I keep going.

Franklin pulls away from me and looks into my eyes. We share a moment.

He glances down at my lips and I look at his. He makes a move to kiss me. Now, I have to decide. Do I let him and tell him that it's okay? Or do I dare to say no?

"Can I kiss you?" he asks.

I press my feet as much into the floor as possible, hoping that it will just open up and swallow me whole.

Sensing my hesitation, he says, "I don't usually ask but I thought that I would give you that courtesy since you are… my wife."

There's hopefulness in his voice. It's almost as though he knows that I won't be able to refuse.

"No," I say.

My word is barely audible but Franklin hears it. He shakes his head, darting his eyes away from me.

"Why do you have to be like that?" he demands.

"Like what?"

"The way you are. Why does everything have to be so *difficult*?"

"Why is this difficult?" I ask. "You asked me if you could kiss me and I said no."

"That's not what I'm talking about and you know it," he says. "I want to get close to you. I want to fuck you. And you? You don't want that?"

I shake my head no.

"Why not?"

"I didn't want to marry you, Franklin, but you insisted. So, here we are. I'm your wife. You asked me if you could kiss me and I said no. Now it's up to you."

"What is?" he asks.

"Will you kiss me despite the fact that I said no?"

He glares at me. His brows furrow and his irises become tiny like pinholes. I can feel his rage building and I take a deep breath and prepare myself for impact.

"What the fuck?!" Franklin roars.

He raises his hand in the air but instead of hitting me, he punches the wall. I flinch and move away from him. He catches me and pushes me up against the wall.

He puts his hand around my neck and squeezes.

I start to gag.

I can't take a breath and my head starts to feel

like it's about to explode. When everything begins to go black, he lets go and I drop onto the floor.

"You're a fucking bitch, you know that? One of these days you're going to get what's coming to you!"

Franklin raises his hand again and I lift my arms to block his blow but instead of hitting me, he hits the pillow.

When he leaves, Franklin slams the door on his way out. Through the tears flowing down my cheeks, I look over at the dresser.

There, right next to the vase with freshly cut roses, I see that he has forgotten his Starbucks cup.

I force myself to my feet, still shaken, and carefully place the cup into a Ziploc bag that I fish out of my purse.

20

AURORA

I meet up with Jackie the following day. We meet up alone without Henry and that's at my request. It's a nondescript diner, one that I chose because no one I know ever goes here.

I get here early and take a seat. I'm hungry so I order a stack of pancakes. The waitress is a tired woman in her forties with thinning hair and sallow skin. She offers me coffee with free refills but I opt for an Earl Grey instead.

Jackie arrives a few minutes late and apologizes profusely. I wave my hand at him and tell him that it doesn't matter.

It doesn't. I like having this time to think. The diner is empty since we're meeting at the dead time between lunch and dinner when few people bother with restaurants.

"Why isn't Henry here?" Jackie asks, getting right to the point.

I swallow hard and look up at him. His eyes are weary and he looks like he didn't sleep last night.

"Are you okay?" I ask.

He nods and says, "I don't look that great, do I?"

"I didn't mean anything by it," I say.

"I worked on a stake-out all last night following this husband who has been screwing around on his wife. She knows he's doing it. I know he's doing it and yet I couldn't catch them in the act."

"Maybe he's not?" I ask.

"Let me tell you, around 6:30 this morning after sitting in front of the building for five hours, I started to think that, too, but then I saw him come out of a one-star hotel with his arm around his girlfriend and he gave her a big wet kiss right for my camera."

"I'm not sure if your work is extremely interesting or extremely boring," I say, taking a sip of my tea.

"A little bit of both."

My pancakes arrive and it's way more than I

can eat. Luckily, Jackie is happy to oblige. He puts a few on his plate, smothering them in maple syrup. I bite into mine completely dry.

"No syrup for you?" Jackie asks.

I shake my head no.

"To answer your question," I say, "things are a little bit complicated now but I wanted to get you this cup. It's in my purse."

"You got it? Already?"

I nod.

"That was fast."

"I want this to end sometime soon. The sooner the better."

"Everyone does but that's not how investigations usually go." Jackie takes another big bite, chewing with his mouth open.

"You don't like me, do you?" I ask.

"I wouldn't say that."

"I'm giving you this investigation on an open platter. I'm doing everything and you seem to be…inconvenienced."

"It's not that," he says, narrowing his eyes. "I appreciate you doing all of *this*."

"So, what's the problem?"

"You. You and Henry," he says after a long pause.

"How's that?" I ask.

"You come from a different world and we both know that and he knows that but there's another part of him that sort of doesn't."

I look down at my fork and watch the light streaming through the window bounce off one of the prongs.

"I don't owe you an explanation," I say.

"No, you don't."

Still, I feel the need to continue.

"I never kept any secrets from him. He knew who I was and I knew who he was. We tried to make it work and we still want to."

"Aren't you married?" Jackie asks.

"I know but I'm not married-married. It wasn't my choice. Didn't Henry tell you?"

"He did but I don't believe him."

"I don't know what I can do to convince you."

"What happened to your face?" Jackie asks.

My heart skips a beat but I don't let it bother me. I'm wearing a lot of makeup and I have camouflaged it well.

"Nothing. Why?"

"Did Franklin do that?" Jackie asks. "Is that why you're after him?"

"Franklin and I aren't together. This whole marriage is and has been a lie from the beginning."

"If that was the case, then why would he beat you up?"

"Are you seriously asking me this?" I lean over the table and hiss at him. He nods.

"Franklin is fucked up," I say after a moment. "Why else would he wanna make a deal for Tate Media and include me in the process? I'm not *with* him. I just have to be with him and you need to do your *fucking* job to make sure no one else gets hurt."

Jackie narrows his eyes and leans back. He watches me. He assesses me, trying to figure out if I'm telling the truth.

"I had no idea that you suspected me of anything," I say after a pause.

"I do," he says nonchalantly. "You're one of the 1% of the 1%. You're the whole reason this country is so fucked up. I don't know what your angle is but I know what people like *you* are capable of and that's pretty much anything."

I shake my head, unwilling to believe what he's saying.

"So, why the fuck are you here? I mean, if you don't believe me, if you think that I'm just playing a game, why are you even helping?"

"I'm here for Henry. He asked me to help so I'm here."

I take my fork and swirl it around the empty plate, collecting all of the crumbs.

"What happened to your face?" he asks.

"I fell," I say, glaring into his eyes.

He shakes his head and a loose strand of hair falls into his face. Our eyes interlock, neither of us daring to blink or look away first.

"Did you want to meet here so that Henry wouldn't see that he's still hurting you?" Jackie asks after a long pause.

"You're a lot smarter than you look," I say with a laugh.

I reach into my purse and pull out Franklin's cup.

"I got you this, now go make me a fake print so I can get into his fucking laptop."

21

AURORA

I haven't seen my mother for a while. Not since the wedding. I don't want to meet up with her but the days are long and sometimes it's nice just to fill them with something.

With the relationship, I feel like I have no identity but it's worse than that. I feel like there's nothing I can do or spend my time on that's worthwhile. Yet I have all of these hours in the day that I spend worrying instead.

I worry about what's going to happen.

I worry about what might not happen.

There're so many things that are outside of my control. Yet, I know that I wield some power in determining the outcome.

It's hard to explain how bored I really am in

between all of the moments of terror and uncertainty. I don't have school to ground me. I read things but nothing stays in my mind. Everything on the news seems like it's happening to someone else or to people far, far away.

Nothing is relevant.

I know that I'm depressed and that I have to do something to get out of this headspace but what?

"Thank you for finally making the time to see me," my mother says, opening the door to her apartment.

She is dressed in a crisp linen suit. Her hair is professionally blow-dried and not covered in two pounds of dry shampoo like mine.

She looks me up and down, undoubtably taking note of my casual attire that she doesn't approve of; black leggings, a loose-fitting sweater that falls off the shoulder, and sneakers.

"I see that you're not spending all of your days primping and beautifying yourself for your new husband," she jokes.

She has a dark sense of humor but sometimes it hits just the right note.

The truth is that I miss her. Before we had this marriage stuck in between us, we could at least talk to one another. I know that we are different people with completely different viewpoints on just about everything but as far as entertaining dinner companions, she's one of the best out there.

"How are you?" I ask, plopping down on her custom-made chiffon sofa that you can't look at sideways without marking it up.

She glances down at my feet to make sure that they don't come anywhere near the cushions. They don't. I have been trained well after all the years of living in this museum.

"I'm good," she says. "Your father is feeling better and, as you know, health is the most important thing."

"Well, I wouldn't say that. There are a few other things you seem to care a whole lot about," I think to myself, looking around at all the sculptures and relics all around the home.

"I'm happy about that," I say. "How about the other thing? The legal situation?"

"Everything seems to be fine there also," she says with a smile. "Thanks to you."

There's no more fear in her eyes.

She's calm, collected, and in control just like she always was when I was growing up. Her hands are folded in her lap and her ankles are crossed.

She's the epitome of poise. If she feels uncertain or confused about anything, she's not letting on.

She's always been like this and for many years I felt like I was growing up with an ice sculpture for a mother.

"How is Franklin?" Mom asks. "We should really have you two over for dinner sometime."

"He's fine," I say. "Very busy with the buyout. So, we probably won't be able to make it anytime soon."

"Oh, I know all about that," Mom says. "There were years that your father and I hardly saw each other at all even though we worked in the same building and slept together in the same apartment."

She says this with a sense of pride that makes me want to gag.

Don't you know that life isn't supposed to be like that?

Doesn't she know that a good life is one that's spent with the people you love?

When I was thirteen and I asked them why we never spent time together when I was a kid, my parents said that they didn't like children much. Nothing changed much over the years. I guess they don't like adults either.

"So, what's the end game here, Mom?" I ask.

Her eyes dart up at me. This is the first bit of emotion that I have seen since I got here and I kind of like it. It reminds me that underneath the façade, she's actually human.

"What are you talking about, Aurora?" she asks.

"Exactly that," I say, leaning back against the back of the couch. "Franklin and I are married. He's going to own Tate Media. What's my exit strategy?"

"So, you two aren't getting along?"

I look up at the ceiling and pretend to consider the possibility but then shake my head.

On the way here, I had thought that perhaps we could talk about something real. Maybe even connect like a mother and daughter should but then I saw the way that she was dressed and her demeanor and her general standoffishness.

I realized that this would be nothing but a game of pretend. I could go along with it, improvise, and make nice or I could make it interesting.

"I have walked in on my husband in bed with two women on two different occasions. He comes into my room and threatens me. He has punched me a few times in fits of rage. Also, choked me until I almost passed out. Luckily, he hasn't raped me yet."

I wasn't expecting to tell her all of this, it all came tumbling out as soon as I opened my mouth. All of this is because of her. It's because of what she and my father asked me to do as a fucking favor.

"Are you saying this to shock me?" Mom asks.

I think about that question for a moment and shake my head no.

"Then I don't understand what you're doing."

"I want you to know what kind of marriage your daughter has. It's definitely not a happy one."

"Anyone can be happy, Aurora."

I wait for her to continue but she doesn't.

"I have no idea what you're talking about," I say.

"Marriage is what you make of it. It requires work. It's two people coming together and agreeing to a certain set of norms. The kind of things you allow to happen in the marriage and the kind of things that you don't."

"Okay, I'll think about that next time he's choking me," I say sarcastically. "Should I talk to him about that right now or should it be a little obvious that I don't wanna fucking get choked?"

"Aurora, you have always made things so complicated. Have you ever thought about the fact that if you just went along and made him feel a little bit more like a man then he wouldn't be cheating on you? That maybe he wouldn't be so angry all the time."

"What do you mean?" I ask.

"You know what I mean," she says. "You said you've never even slept with him. So, you two are married and you have never consummated your relationship."

"No. So far he has taken no for an answer."

"Maybe that's the whole problem. Maybe all this other stuff is happening because you're not giving your husband what he wants."

I shake my head and stand up. The rage boiling in my core is difficult to describe. Every time that I think that I could possibly reach my mother, she just says something that pushes me farther and farther away.

"Who the fuck are you?" I roar. "How are you saying these things to me? You're my mother. You're supposed to protect me. You're supposed to care about me. I've never felt safe with you. You know what I've always felt? Like I wasn't good enough. That's what *you* made *me* feel."

"I'm thankful for what you're doing. We both are. I don't know where we would be without you. All I'm trying to do is give you some advice.

Franklin is who he is and that's not going to change. So, you have to."

I swallow hard and take a deep breath, breathing slowly. I feel my nostrils flare as I take another breath, then another.

Her calmness is making me angry. All I want to do is grab her by the shoulders and shake her as hard as I can to wake her up.

She's not real. None of what she's saying is real but when my eyes meet hers, I realize that this is exactly who she has been my whole life; cold, distant, and unreachable.

"I'm not doing this for you," I say, gazing directly into her eyes. "I'm not doing this for you or for Dad. I'm doing this for Tate Media and all of those innocent people whose pensions you have squandered. I'm doing this to save my legacy. One of these days that company is gonna become mine and I'm going to run it the right way, if it's the last thing I do."

22

HENRY

I work late in the office and don't get home until after ten. On the drive back, my thoughts oscillate between Aurora and my mom, two women whose predicaments I cannot control or influence in any way.

I know that Aurora told me to not stand up for her in front of Franklin. That promise is harder to keep than I ever imagined. I don't see him much in the office but when I do, our interactions are personal. I'm usually the only one there and he often wants to share a drink. He asks about my mom and about my work. He is genuinely interested or maybe he is actually pretending to be.

It's hard to imagine that this is the same person who has put his hand on the woman I love, multiple times. It's almost as if he's an actor, a ghost. The person I see is not who she sees and neither of us are the person that he presents to the public.

So far, I have kept my promise to her, because I'm doing it for the greater good. That video that she showed me made me sick to my stomach and he needs to pay for everything that he has done. The only way that he will do that is if we gather more evidence.

What is on that laptop?

Who else is there with him?

How many other politicians are involved besides the governor?

If I confront him about Aurora, if I throw a punch, we won't get answers to any of these questions. Those people will keep getting away with it and those girls will never get the justice they deserve.

All of this stuff weighs heavily on my mind as I pull into the familiar driveway of my mother's house. It's an old house that needs a lot of improvements that my mother could never afford but the only reason that it is still in the family is because of Franklin. I sent her whatever money I have, but it is his check that has saved this home for us. I'm not saying that I'm not thankful for that or that I'm not conflicted over the kindness that he has shown me.

I sneak into the house, walking on my tiptoes, and trying not to make a sound. My mom is probably already asleep or at least trying to get there. She's an insomniac and once she's woken up, she will often spend hours unable to get back to sleep. Her diagnosis, all the worries about her prognosis, and how she's going to pay for everything do not help in easing her mind.

"Hey, you're back!" Mom startles me, getting off the couch.

"Oh my God," I say. "I didn't mean to wake you up. What are you doing here?"

Mom has a TV in her room and a very comfortable bed that I had splurged on a few years ago just to give her as much rest as possible. I don't remember the last time I saw her on the couch at night. This is usually my domain.

"I was waiting up for you," she says. "I wanted to tell you this in person."

My mouth drops open but I force it closed. My heart starts palpitating and I grab onto the chair to steady myself.

I can't handle anymore bad news today but I

don't have a choice. The only thing I can control is how I react to it.

"Okay," I say, quietly bracing myself for something like 'it's spread' or 'it doesn't look good.'

"They called me and they said that we have contained it. It's in remission. Well, they didn't use the word remission because that has some specific medical definition but it's good news. I still have to go back for tests every two months and then every three and six, but for now, it's all good."

She's talking so fast and saying so many things, that I can barely process it all.

"Wait? So, it's better? You're better?"

"I am in remission. For now, we just have to wait and see."

She starts talking again but all I can do is pull her close to me and wrap my arms around her frail body.

I let out a sigh of relief and tears well up in my eyes. I can't believe the good news. I ask her to repeat herself over and over again just to make sure that I'm not dreaming.

"Nothing is set in stone, of course, they're gonna have to monitor the situation and I have to go in for more tests and probably do more chemo for maintenance. But this is really good news,

Henry. I wouldn't be here without you," she says, hugging me.

With her arms around me, I can tell how much stronger she is now. Suddenly, I remember all of those other moments when I was with her when she laughed and wasn't as tired as she was before.

They're all symptoms that this is true. I want to celebrate but another part of me doesn't want to jinx it.

I will not live in fear, I decide.

I go to the bottom drawer of our kitchen cabinets, the one Dad used as a backup pantry to the cabinet above. This is where we keep all the stuff that we don't usually need all the time like backup cans of soup and beans and other non-perishables.

In the back, I find a bottle of champagne that I bought a few years ago and told her that we would open when we have something momentous to celebrate.

"No, no, no," Mom says, waving her hand at me. "We can't open this now."

"We have to," I say. "This is the best news that we've gotten …ever. Even if it's temporary, even if something changes, we have to celebrate *today*. We have to acknowledge this moment and be present."

My mom continues to protest, saying that the bottle should be kept for something a lot more significant but her protests are no longer that insistent. I know that she agrees with me.

You would be surprised but I don't have that much experience opening champagne bottles and as soon as I pop the cork, the foam spills onto the floor, adding to the celebration. My mom laughs as I try to catch it into our glasses, rather unsuccessfully.

"This is the best news that I could get," I say, raising my glass to hers. "You are a wonderful mother and you have always been there for me. I just wish that I could be there for you."

"You have been," she says. "I love you, son."

Her voice cracks at the end and when I say I love you, too, mine does as well. We wipe our tears, slightly embarrassed by them but not enough to actually pretend that they're not coming.

"Let's make this glass the beginning of something wonderful," I continue. "A new life, for both of us."

"I want to say something, too," she says as I'm about to put down my glass. I raise it back up.

"You're the best son that any mother could ever hope for," she says. "You have always been there for me, even when you probably should not have. I never wanted to be a burden to you. I just wanted to raise you and watch you become the man that you are, the man that I always knew you could be. Now that I'm better, I want you to stop worrying about me. I want you to promise me that. I want you to stop worrying and I want you to focus on you."

"Me?"

"You have a lot of things going on in your life and they need a lot of figuring out. Mainly, it's that woman that you're in love with that you can't get out of your head."

I swallow hard and look down at my feet.

"I want you to make it right with Aurora," Mom says. "I know that she can make you happy and I know that you can make her happy. I just hope that you two can figure things out before it's too late."

23

AURORA

The following afternoon, Henry and I make the arrangements to meet up through a burner phone that I bought at Walmart. If Franklin catches me with it, I know that whatever trust he has in me will disappear immediately. But I have to have a way to talk to Henry, for real and in private.

On the way to the hotel, I make sure that no one is following me by examining every unknown face. I had promised myself that if I suspect that I am being trailed by anyone at all that I'm going to call this off. I don't think I can handle the wrath that Franklin would impose on me if he were to find out the truth.

Henry paid for the room and I take the elevator

up to the third floor. It's a nondescript, three-star hotel that caters to business travelers. They only allow check-ins after three in the afternoon and I get there a few minutes later. I can't stay out too late. I have to be back at the apartment before Franklin gets back.

Henry pulls me into his arms as soon as he opens the door. He presses his lips to mine and my whole body starts to shiver. I drop my bag onto the floor and wrap my arms around him.

His hands make their way up my shirt and unclasp my bra. He pushes me against the wall. I kiss him, desperately searching for his tongue. His hands make their way around my stomach, cupping my breasts. I turn my head back when he squeezes. A fire is ignited in the middle of my core, the kind that I have forgotten that I still have.

"I've missed you," he mumbles through his sloppy kiss.

"I've missed you, too," I whisper.

He leads me to the bedroom, holding my hand firmly in his. He's wearing a tight, white T-shirt that accentuates every protruding muscle in his torso.

I watch the way his six pack moves up and down with each breath. When he throws me on the bed, I lick my lips in anticipation and pull off his shirt. The room is dark but there is candlelight streaming from the hallway. It's not a real candle but it flickers and behaves like one.

I stare at it as he kisses my lips and my neck. I arch my back as he pulls off my shirt and my bra.

Finally, we are flesh to flesh. I glance at him and run my fingers down his hard body. His abs are a perfect six-pack, almost as if he is photo shopped.

"How do you have this...body?" I ask, letting my fingers go up and down his torso, around the sides of his stomach, where his muscles form the letter V, as if they are an arrow directing me to his beautiful cock.

I tug at his belt buckle and let it fall open on to my stomach.

"I tend to lift weights when I get frustrated," he says, kissing behind my ear. "Recently, I've been frustrated a lot."

"So, when we're finally together, you're going to let yourself go?" I ask.

"If you want," Henry says, pulling away from me just a little bit.

"I want you any way I can have you," I say.

He smiles, kisses me again, and flips over on his back.

"Come lie on top of me," he says.

This feels good. Powerful. But then he pulls down on me, folding my body in half.

He kisses me again and again, fondling my breasts. Even with me on top, he's in charge. I like that.

I don't like that in most of my life, but right here and now, it feels beautiful just like him.

I trust him.

He won't hurt me.

In fact, he'll make me feel the kind of pleasure that I can only dream of.

Pulling off my pants, I lean on top of him as he kisses my neck, my breasts, and my stomach. He keeps pushing me further and finally I don't want to say no.

He pulls me up to his mouth, I sit on him and he buries his fingers and his tongue deep within me. I grip the headboard and lose myself in the moment. His fingers move expertly around me quickly getting me to that place from which there's no turning back.

I start to moan. I feel a wave coming over me and before I realize what's happening, he gets behind me and thrusts himself inside. His dick is hard and thick and fills every aspect of me, finally making me feel complete.

"Henry!" I whisper his name, unable to create an audible sound.

One wave crashes followed by another and my body seems to take over. We move as one, together as if we were made this way. With each thrust, he goes deeper and deeper inside and I consume more and more of him.

The final wave comes and I curl my toes. It's warm and soothing as it explodes from the center of my core, reverberating all around.

I shake, moving myself up and down harder and harder to try to make it last longer. Somewhere behind me, I hear him moan my name and thrust one last time.

We hold each other for a long time after that, grasping to one another, breathing deeply but unable to catch our breaths.

"I really miss you," Henry says, staring at the ceiling.

He's somewhere far away and so am I, but in a good way.

"I've missed you, too," I say, squeezing his hand.

"I have to tell you something," he says.

I shake my head no and say, "I don't wanna hear any bad news right now. I just can't…"

I know that I'm being selfish. He probably

wants to tell me about his mom but not just yet. I will be here for him and I will hold him and I will tell him that everything will be okay but I can't do that just yet. I need this moment to last a little longer to replenish my dwindling supplies of optimism.

"It's not what you think. Her cancer is in remission."

I turn to face him.

Did I hear that correctly?

"They still have to wait and see and she has to go in for lots of tests every few months to make sure that it doesn't come back but it's gone." There's a tear in the corner of his eye. I bring my finger to it and wipe it.

"I'm so happy," I say, kissing him softly on the lips. "I'm so… she's going to be okay."

I let out a deep sigh of relief. I had only met her a few times but she's a kindred soul, the kind that is rare in this world.

I didn't want Henry to lose her. I didn't want to lose her.

24

AURORA

Franklin gets home later that evening and I have a martini waiting for him, like a good 1950s housewife. He takes it, gives me a small peck on the cheek, and downs it.

"Hard day?" I ask.

He goes straight to his closet and changes out of his clothes. When he emerges, he is dressed in sweats and has a defeated look on his face.

"What's going on?" I ask.

"Your father… He is just so difficult."

He wrestles with his thoughts before saying the word and I know that he had considered a few alternatives.

"You mean, he's an asshole?" I ask, taking a sip of my own martini.

"Well, I wasn't going to say that but there you go."

"I could've told you that. What happened?"

"There's just all this shit with the buyout. He has all these demands. He wants to hold onto a big portion of it, and a bunch of others. It wouldn't interest you."

I move my jaw slightly from one side to another and ball up my fists. I'm sitting next to him but my hands are buried behind me in the couch, out of sight.

"What would make you think that it wouldn't interest me?" I ask. "I'm interested in Tate Media. It is my parents' company."

"Well, not anymore."

"Did my father sign all the paperwork?"

He doesn't answer. He knows what I'm getting at so I don't push.

"So, what does he want?" I ask. "Now, you have piqued my interest."

"More ownership of the shares. More control, what does anyone want?"

I'm about to question him some more when he changes the subject.

"So, what's going on with you? Any plans for the future?"

I shrug and lean back into the sofa. It wraps around me like a thick warm shawl but the comfort that I feel is only an illusion.

"I don't know what you're talking about," I say.

"We haven't talked for a while, so I was just wondering what you wanna do with your life. You got your PhD. What are your plans now?"

The lines of concern between his two eyebrows relaxes and he looks at me with the face of someone who is genuinely interested.

"To tell you the truth, I have no idea. It's hard to explain but I don't really know what's going on. Maybe I'm feeling a little bored. Maybe depressed but I don't have another project lined up. I don't have another class to take and so, I'm sort of…listless?"

"That's a standardized test word," he says with a smile.

I nod.

"Yeah, I may know one or two big words but what does that matter? What does that get me?"

"Listen, you are the daughter of parents who have built one of the biggest media empires in the world who is now married to a man who has acquired it and you can't find a job? Well, then we have a real problem on our hands as a society."

I laugh. I can't help it. I don't want to but the giggles just come out. You can say a lot of things about Franklin but you cannot say that he's not charming.

"Seriously, though, do you want a job?" he asks.

"Is this what this is about?" I ask. "I mean, is this why you think I'm feeling a little depressed?"

"Well," he says, spreading his arms around the back of the sofa and lifting his ankle onto one knee. "I have to tell you, not having something to do during the day is one of the major causes of depression. Everyone's going to work. Everyone's trying to achieve something and you're just hanging around."

"Are you saying that I'm being lazy?" I ask.

"No, I really don't want to imply that," he says quickly. "If you don't wanna have a job and you want to be a stay-at-home wife, you want to pursue a hobby, or just hang out with friends, that's perfectly fine with me. God knows we have the money but the thing that I was getting at is that you just don't seem to be the type. You don't know what to do with yourself. You like to work hard, otherwise you wouldn't have gotten your PhD without anyone's support. You like to pursue meaningful work and you shouldn't apologize for that."

"Would that be okay with you?" I ask.

He looks me up and down and nods his head.

"Of course. It would be more than okay. I would love it. That place is a shark tank and I need people on my side. Besides, I think the employees of Tate Media would appreciate having one of their own on board."

I give him a slight nod.

"I really appreciate this," I say, looking at him and taking his hand in mine. He glances down and waits for me to squeeze it.

This is probably the most genuine connection I've ever experienced with my husband up until this point.

He's right, of course. I should have done this long ago. I'm not the type to do nothing and I don't have many hobbies or interests outside of work.

"I've never felt welcome at that company with my parents being in charge," I say after a long pause. "They were very controlling and everything had to be just so. Other people could make mistakes but I couldn't. I was their daughter and I guess if I made mistakes it meant that they were making mistakes."

"It doesn't have to be that way."

"I hope not. I only worked there as an intern

one summer and I couldn't handle it, not because of the work or the people but because of their micromanaging and second-guessing. I didn't just report to my immediate superior, I had to also report up to *them* and… it just made everything unsuitable."

"That's not what I want this relationship to be," Franklin says. "I don't want to control you. I definitely don't want that in the workplace."

"So, you're not going to watch my every move?" I ask.

He shakes his head no and says, "I trust you. Also, I know that you only have Tate Media's best interests at heart. I will not get involved with anything unless there's a real dispute that I have to get to the bottom of."

I think about the proposition and I like it. I love writing, I love words, and I love telling stories.

"So, what would I do there?" I ask.

"What do you want to do?" he asks. "Do you want to work in corporate? Oversee personnel, manage the kind of stories that we tell? Do you want to be the one who's actually telling the stories? The crime division is doing well but that's probably the one place you can't get a position."

Our eyes meet and he gives me a little wink.

I smile back, at the corner of my lips.

"Why is that?" I ask. "Is it because my ex-boyfriend, Henry Asher, runs one of the most successful podcasts in your crime division?"

"Yeah, I think it has something to do with that," he says sarcastically.

I can't blame him for this restriction. In fact, I am surprised at his generosity. Never in a million years did I think that he would actually make this offer. Never in a million years did I think that he would want me to work at his company.

"I really appreciate this," I say. "I hope you know how genuine I am when I say that."

"It will be a pleasure to have you there and to spend more time with you," Franklin says. "I'm sure that I will be able to find the right fit for you."

I shake my head, reach over, and give him a hug.

"I really appreciate this," I whisper into his chest.

I truly do. What is not lost on me, however, is how conflicted I feel about him as a person.

I know that one nice word or one good deed doesn't make up for all of the bad things that he has done, but it does affect the conflict that I feel inside.

Franklin gives me these glimpses of goodness

that make me wonder why the bad exists in the first place. How can he be both of these things at the same time?

When I pull away from him, I lean back and look into his eyes. I feel him watching me but his gaze is different this time. Something is different. Something has shifted.

"Why don't you spend the night with me? In our bedroom?" he asks.

25

AURORA

My blood runs cold and I feel my whole body withdraw from him but there's something different in his eyes this time. He doesn't make a move toward me. There's a casualness in his demeanor. He doesn't have that glint in his eyes that he had when he tried to touch me before. It puts me at ease but at the same time it throws me off.

What does he want?

"Don't look at me like that," Franklin says. "I'm not a monster."

I shake my head, instinctively. I don't want him to think that I think that.

"You don't have to do anything you don't want

to do," he says, keeping the tone of his voice as calm as possible.

"So…why?"

"Because, I want to sleep with you. Is that so wrong?"

"Sleep with you?" I ask in a barely audible whisper.

"I'm tired of sleeping alone, Aurora. I'm married. I just want someone there. Someone breathing next to me. Can you understand that?"

I give him a slight nod. A few loose strands of hair fall into my face as I exhale slowly. I understand that more than he could possibly know.

I cautiously believe him but keep my guard up. I don't dare say no. So far, he has been more than gracious and understanding.

We walk to the master bedroom and my feet make a loud creaking sound on the polished hardwood floors.

"Do you need anything from your room?" he asks.

I do, so I stop by and grab my phone along with my eye mask and earphones.

"Do you sleep with your AirPods in?" Franklin asks.

"Yes," I say.

He smiles. "So do I."

"I usually sleep naked," Franklin says, "but I don't want to make you uncomfortable."

I'm about to disagree but instead I just thank him.

"How about you?" he asks.

"Sweats, kind of like these."

He heads to the marble bathroom to brush his teeth and wash his face. I haven't done any of that yet but I get into bed anyway. I can only bear to take baby steps with this and going through my whole evening ritual right now, let alone doing that in front of him feels like it would be too personal.

Franklin doesn't comment on this. Instead, he just gets into bed next to me and opens this phone. By clicking on the app, the lights dim and my heart skips a beat. Is this when it's going to happen? Is this when he will turn on me and make his move?

I open the Kindle app on my phone and stare at the words of the book that I have been reading or rather *not* reading for the last week. I read the same sentence over and over again but it's no more comprehensible.

Out of the corner of my eye, I feel him watching me. My mind starts to race but I don't dare move.

"Good night," he says and shuts off the light above his head.

The dim light above mine remains. It's controlled by my phone and I quickly search for the app to turn it off. Somehow, I feel like I will be safer in the dark.

"You don't have to go to sleep on my account," Franklin says. "Feel free to keep reading."

"Okay," I say after a long pause.

I hear him starting to move and get comfortable. When I glance over, I see him with his face turned away from me, and his arms firmly hugging his pillow.

"Aurora," he says, his voice muffled.

"Yeah?" I whisper, tensing my toes and praying that this isn't all an elaborate set-up for the sudden attack.

"Thank you for staying here tonight. It feels really good to have you with me."

I don't respond. My body relaxes and I let out a long sigh of relief but with the next breath, I feel a pang of guilt as well.

I READ for a few hours until I am certain that he is

asleep. After that, I wait even more. I listen to his breathing and I hear him falling deeper and deeper into sleep. Finally, around two in the morning, I gather enough courage to slip out of bed.

I tiptoe over to his office where he left his laptop and pull out the copy of the thumbprint that Jackie dropped off with me. We met at a coffee shop and he slipped it into my purse saying that all I have to do is adhere the thumbprint to my own and press down.

I don't know what's going to happen or even if it will work. I also don't know what's going to happen to the laptop if it shows that it has a failed login.

Will there be a report of these attempts?

Suddenly, I wonder if this is the stupidest thing I have ever done in my life.

No, it's not. Marrying Franklin was.

I adhere the sticker to my thumb and count to three.

"One. Two. Three."

Okay, you were supposed to press your thumb print and unlock the computer but I didn't.

I simply stay here, frozen in space.

I take another deep breath.

And then another.

All of the courage that you had up until this point is not worth shit if you don't go through with it, I say to myself.

Instead of counting again, I just go for it. I press my thumb down and a little circle pops up with an arrow going around in a clockwise motion. A moment later, I'm in.

26

AURORA

Another part of my brain takes over. I search the computer efficiently and without hesitation. I don't know how much time I have, so I work fast. I don't bother to look back and I don't bother to worry about whether or not Franklin is still sleeping. If he catches me here, it's all over. There's no way to explain. There are no amends to make.

Surprisingly, he is such an arrogant bastard, that the files are hidden in a folder that's called 'Others.' There are only two folders on the desktop but it takes me a few minutes to find them.

The video files are not named but numbered so I start at the beginning. I click on the first one and I see that it's an ex-president with an underage boy and a girl with the same set-up as before. A massage table is there. They are told what to do. Tears are in their eyes along with far away looks and deadpan expressions.

I fast forward through it. I'm not here to analyze or watch. I'm here just to transfer it to an external hard drive and take it somewhere else for safekeeping.

The second video is focused on a man I don't immediately recognize. I have seen his face on C-SPAN, but I can't quite place him. The third is a lobbyist for the coal industry. The only reason I know who he is, is because he wrote a pretty famous book denying the effects of climate change.

I transfer each video without examining the contents carefully. They are on his computer and they're there for a reason. Franklin is holding onto them as leverage. None of these men want this to come out and none of them know that they are being recorded.

How many of these men think that their secrets are safe?

How much would they pay Franklin to never have these videos come out?

How quickly will they turn on him?

How likely is Franklin to release them?

I have no intentions of making myself rich or richer by keeping these people's secrets. I promise myself here now that every last one of them is going to go down and be exposed for what they have done, along with my husband.

There is only one disinfectant for a lie and that is sunlight.

I transfer one video after another to my thumb drive. We have fast internet but this is still a time-consuming process. When I get to the last video, suddenly a thought pops into my head and tilts my world on its axis.

What if my father is one of these men?

There's one video left and I hold my breath when opening it. It never occurred to me before that my father could be one of these people but now it seems like the most obvious thing in the world.

He's the CEO and founder of one of the most influential media companies the world has ever seen. Franklin's little video collection has just about everyone else implicated and what they have done, what if he's there, too?

I click on the last video and look for his face but I don't see him. The suit that is featured is older than him, much fatter and unfamiliar to me. I copy that video over and close the laptop. I sit here for a few moments holding the drive as if it's the most precious thing I own.

It is.

After taking a few moments to celebrate silently in my head, I open the laptop again and go through the files. I need to make sure that whatever is on here, I see. I go through each folder carefully, clicking on and opening files, no matter what it's called or how it's labeled. I focus on the ones that are videos and images.

At the bottom of one folder, beneath files of Excel sheets, I find another video entitled 3112. I click on it and my mouth drops open. I watch it once and then I watch it again to be certain if I'm seeing everything right.

"Could this be it?" I ask myself.

No, this can't be true. I've seen the real video on the news a million times. They had it in circulation and they showed it over and over again but this video, it's so different. It has been altered.

Why would Franklin have a copy of this one but not the other one?

I sit on the edge of the chair, trying to figure out what is happening. Unlike the other videos that I have downloaded, this one is innocuous enough.

There's no sex in it. No powerful men. You wouldn't think that there's anything interesting about it at all except for what it shows.

This has been a news story for a few months. It's a video recording of a self-driving car that exploded right in the middle of the intersection. After this video became public, they showed it on the news over and over again, eventually inciting fear in consumers and halting the production of the cars.

In one frame, the car is driving along the road and another it simply explodes as if someone had rigged it to blow up. No one got hurt, luckily but that didn't stop all of the talking heads on television from spewing their so-called concerns. The story had caught on and it was like that missing airliner in Malaysia, everyone wanted to know what happened.

But this video is different.

It's not the one they keep showing on the news. It's the same car at the same intersection and everything about it is exactly the same except that there's *no explosion*.

. . .

IT DOESN'T SEEM like it would be a big deal. One altered video about some self-driving car.

Who cares, right?

The thing is that if this video, the one that Franklin has on his computer, is true, then the one that the public has seen is nothing but a fabrication.

And that's a very, very big deal.

I tiptoe back to bed and climb in next to him. I spend the rest of the night in a restless state, unable to sleep.

I keep tossing and turning over my thoughts that keep returning to one thing. The videos of the sex abuse are terrible and all of those men are going to pay for what they did, but it's the self-driving car that I keep thinking about. The only way that I can get answers is if I go straight to the source.

27

AURORA

The following morning, Franklin gets up early and heads to work. I wait until he leaves to make an appointment to have lunch with my dad. I wear a suit and show up prepared. I have the video itself isolated and saved onto my phone. He has some explaining to do and the best way that I can get to the truth is to confront him with it.

As soon as I walk in, my father tells me that he 'doesn't have much time.' He looks frazzled and out of control, like something heavy is weighing on his mind.

"What's going on?" I ask.

"I don't know. You tell me," he says, rubbing his temples.

I wish that he would be relaxed, calm, and at ease, but I guess this will have to do.

"What's going on with that husband of yours?" my dad asks.

"What are you talking about?"

"We had an agreement. We had agreed on a price. We had agreed on a share. We had agreed on…you. It was our only reason why I decided to give him that much. Now, suddenly, he wants to go back on his word."

"What is he saying?" I ask, hoping that I can get more information from him than I can get from Franklin.

"Are you in on this?" Dad asks me straight on.

I shake my head no and add, "Absolutely not. I don't really know what's going on. Tell me."

"He's going back on his word. He wants more. Another fifteen percent. That was not what we discussed."

I shrug my shoulders, unsure as to what to say. They have kept me out of all of the negotiations and I am as much in the dark as anyone else.

"I'm sick of these games, Aurora. You better talk to him."

"I don't know what's going on," I say. "He won't

tell me anything and you never did. Do you want my help? If so, then you need to fill me in."

Dad looks at me, narrowing his eyes. He breathes heavily and his nostrils flare from anger.

"I have something that I wanna show you," I say. "I want you to tell me what it means."

"I don't have time for this, Aurora."

"Yes, you do," I say as calmly as possible.

I take out my phone and click on the video app then I play him the doctored video.

He doesn't look away and watches the whole thing. I, on the other hand, watch his face turn pale and all blood drain out of it.

"Everyone in the world saw that self-driving car blow up and nearly kill someone. It was played over and over and all the primetime shows and discussed it ad nauseam on all the daytime ones."

"I have no idea what this is," he says, after some of the shock wears off.

I shake my head no and say, "Yes, you do."

He gets up from behind the oak table and paces in front of me. He walks back-and-forth and then back-and-forth again.

Slowly, deliberately.

I see him thinking. I know him well enough to

realize that I'm onto something. He knew about this video but why?

"What does this mean?" I ask.

He doesn't answer.

"That video you ran on all of your networks is fake," I say. "You know it."

Again, he doesn't respond.

"You're not going to explain yourself?" I ask.

"I don't owe you an explanation," my father responds.

There's that anger that I have been searching for. Now all of my suspicions are confirmed. He knew that he was running a fake video. He knew it all along.

"You made that video legitimate by running it on the network and having all of the pundits talk about it all the time. People are afraid of self-driving cars now because it spoke to their darkest fears. About technology taking over everything and about technology making all of us obsolete."

"So what?" Dad asks.

"Why? Why did you do this?"

"Why else, Aurora? Why else would someone like me do anything like that?" He's challenging me the way that he used to when I was a kid. Asking me the same questions back so that I will think up my own explanation.

This time, however, I don't have an answer.

"The company, we're going under. Franklin is our only hope. It was the only way that I was going to stave off bankruptcy. Before Franklin was an option, before I knew whether you would agree to marry him and all of his demands would be met, I had to make a contingency plan."

He stops talking. He walks over to the glass bar and pours himself a glass of whiskey. He does not offer me a drink.

"I was strapped for cash," he says, sitting down across from me in the chair in front of his desk. It swivels and he turns to face me.

Now, we are face-to-face. He doesn't sit back, instead he leans forward. He focuses all of his attention on me, and his eyes plead for my forgiveness.

"I borrowed a lot of money from the pension fund," Dad says.

"Borrowed?" I correct him.

"Okay, stole. I wanted to put it back but it just didn't turn out that way. We just kept hemorrhaging money and there was nothing I could do."

"What happened?"

"I took a bribe. A pretty big one but it was the only way that I could hold off going bankrupt and losing everything."

"What was the purpose of that video?" I ask.

"There's a short seller involved. I had to approve the release of the fake video of the test and of the self-driving car blowing up."

"Why?" I ask.

"The short seller had put in the short position on that company's stock. After the video came out, PR5, the company that created the self-driving car, their stock started to fall. The longer that video circulated and the more attention it got especially on primetime, the harder that stock fell. The short seller, he made millions. Probably even a billion."

I shake my head, not wanting to believe what I just heard.

"PR5 was the kind of company that no one thought could ever go under. It was valued so incredibly high and no one thought that anything would happen."

"Well, nothing did. That video is a fake."

"I know but I had to do it."

"How much money did you get from it?"

"A lot," he says.

"I need a specific number."

"At least 400 million, maybe 500. It's still not all in our accounts but it will be."

"So, you're laundering the money on top of that fraud?" I ask.

"Of course, how else do you expect it to come back into our coffers?"

"So, what now?" I ask.

Dad shrugs his shoulders and takes another sip of his whiskey.

"That was major fraud, you know that, right?"

He tilts his head and looks up at me with his big blue eyes. Those were the same eyes that I used to love as a little girl. I grew up adoring him. He could never do anything wrong. He was smart, powerful, and funny. He had every attribute that someone would want to be described as. That was what he was to me when I was a child, but I got older and things changed. Then reality set in.

Perhaps that happens with everyone but mine was particularly small. I realized that he may have told me that he loved me on more than one occasion, probably a lot more than most dads told their children but whether or not he actually did love me, I didn't know for sure. Maybe that's not fair. Maybe he did love me in his own way. In his own selfish, narcissistic, self-centered, and completely egotistical way.

"There's something else, Aurora," Dad says.

"What?"

"The short seller I told you about, Daniel Kavinsky, he threatened my life if this thing with you and Franklin falls apart."

I shake my head no. So, that's it. That's who had threatened to kill him. My mom wasn't lying. She just didn't tell me all of the details.

"Franklin is going down," I say after a moment. "I found some videos that are not going to put him in the best light. He's involved in a lot of things and I'm going to make him pay for it."

"You can't do that, Aurora. He's a very dangerous man. He has connections everywhere—"

"He used to have those connections," I say, smiling at the corner of my lips. "He's been making videos of all of his friends and acquaintances doing sick and perverted things. He's been keeping them as collateral. He's been keeping those videos to try to influence his way to get whatever the hell he wants. Well, I'm going to put a stop to it."

"How?"

"I don't know yet but I'm here telling you this as a courtesy."

My father sits up in his seat. He has never been talked to in this manner before, not by anyone he considers to be inferior to him, least of all his daughter.

I sit up as well and cross my legs from one to the other. I lean over and say, "You need to go to the FBI. You need to tell them what you know. You need to bring a lawyer with you and try to work out some sort of deal."

He shakes his head no.

"I'm taking Franklin and all of those other assholes down. He's going to pay for what he did and they will be exposed for everything they did."

"I'm not gonna go to the FBI. I can't. They won't offer me anything."

"They will if you try to make a deal with them. Bring your lawyer. I'm sure that there's a deal you can make."

He shakes his head no.

"This is the one time that I want you to listen to me," I say quietly but calmly. "They're going to pay for what they did. Like it or not, you're involved with it. I don't want to hurt you and I don't want to put your life in danger. The only way out is to go to the authorities."

"No, absolutely not," Dad says.

28

AURORA

The next time that I meet up with Henry, I tell him what happened. I made copies of everything and hand him the originals to keep for safe keeping. He promises to give them to Jackie.

"How's everything with Franklin?" he asks.

"Fine," I say, not wanting to talk about that. "You make copies of all of this and store them in different places. Give one to Jackie as well. I want there to be a lot of evidence, in case any of it gets lost."

"In case he takes any of it from you, you mean," Henry says. "In case he finds out that you have it."

"Yes, of course. Things are fine right now. We

are actually even friendly but that's because he doesn't know what I know."

Henry breathes deeply.

"There's something else," I say. He waits for me to continue. I open my phone and show him the video of the self-driving car.

He shakes his head. "I've seen that all over the news," he says. "But it was…"

"It was altered," I say. "My father made a fake after he got into an arrangement with a short seller and when the stock dropped, they both made millions. That was major fraud."

Henry shakes his head in disbelief.

"I had no idea that he was capable of something like that."

"Did you talk to him about it?" he asks.

I nod.

I open another app and let him listen to the recording.

"You taped him?" Henry asks.

"I knew that he would deny it. I needed proof. I need him to do the right thing."

"This is very dangerous, Aurora."

"I know," I say. "He doesn't know about the recording yet. I want to get him to go to the FBI and make a deal. I told him that I was very serious about this but he refused."

"What are you gonna do?"

"I don't know but this recording is my leverage. I need your help to come up with a plan to deal with all of this."

We are in a public place, a park, but the place is deserted. We're the only ones here on this evening at twilight. The street lamps are already lit and somewhere in the distance a dog is barking. I reach over and hold his hand. He squeezes mine and makes a move to kiss me but I push him back and shake my head.

"Not here," I whisper. "I don't know who's watching."

I hear his phone vibrate and he pulls it out of his pocket. When he answers it, all the blood drains away from his face and his skin turns a grayish blue color.

"What's wrong?" I mouth to him.

He mouths back, "No" and says, "okay, I'll be right there."

When he hangs up, he stares at the screen for a few moments before turning to me. A lump forms in the back of my throat as I wait for the news.

"It's my mom," he says. "She passed out again. They took her in."

I follow him to the parking structure and get into the passenger seat. He tries to tell me that I don't need to come with him but I can't force myself to stay away.

His mother is unconscious and is in the hospital two hours away from here. I don't want him making the drive by himself or being there when the worst happens, if it were to happen.

Henry doesn't protest much as he is lost somewhere in his thoughts. We don't talk as we sit in Manhattan traffic during rush hour. By the time we get onto Long Island, hours have passed.

"You need to get back," he says when he pulls up to the small community hospital.

"I know but I'm going in with you. I'm going to be here for this."

He doesn't ask me what that is but we both know. I'm worried that this is the end. I'm worried that she's gone.

I hold Henry's hand as we walk in and walk up to the administration desk. The attendant points us in the right direction. My sneakers make a loud squeaking sound on the linoleum floors.

When we get to her room, a doctor comes out

and pulls Henry aside. She is a pretty brunette who is about the same age as we are. I watch her explain something to him, just out of ear shot.

I wonder where she went to school and what my life would be like if I had her job right now. Is she happy?

Does she feel fulfilled waking up every morning and taking care of people?

"Thank you so much." Henry turns around and I see the wave of relief sweep over him. I rush over to him to hear the news.

"We can go inside. She lost consciousness but they have stabilized her. They're not sure what's wrong but for right now… she's okay."

I take a short, cautious breath. This is good news but the ordeal isn't over yet.

"I thought that she was in remission," I say.

"Yeah, me, too," he says with great sorrow in his voice. "I guess we were wrong."

I follow Henry into the hospital room and stay by the door as he sits down on the chair and pulls it closer to his mom. She's unconscious. There are loud machines beeping and breathing for her and I feel incredibly sorry for her and what she and Henry are going through. I wish that there was something I could do.

Maybe she needs another opinion? Maybe she needs to be in a place with better equipment?

I decide to talk to Henry about this when I have a moment but for right now, I just stand here and watch him hold her hand and cry.

I DON'T GO HOME this evening. I stay here with Henry and Mrs. Asher. At first, I debate whether I should come right out and tell Franklin where I am but I decide against it.

Instead, I call Ellis and ask her for a favor. She agrees to tell Franklin that I am with her. She also agrees to reroute her phone call with him if he were to ask to talk to me on the phone. Luckily, neither of these things happen.

When I call Franklin and tell him that Ellis is having a hard time with her boyfriend and has asked me to stay over, he is only too happy to agree. My heart jumps into my throat as I imagine what kind of debauchery, and other stuff he will be up to while I'm gone. Yet another part of me is thankful that he is going to be distracted.

Around 5 o'clock in the morning, just as my body gets too tired to force myself awake anymore sitting in that uncomfortable hospital chair, Henry's mom wakes up. She looks tired, but alert. She even sits up and asks for something to eat. I run off to the cafeteria but it's not open yet, so I make do with the vending machines.

When I come back holding two fruit cups, an apple, and a bag of pretzels, the two of them are actually laughing.

"It's so nice to see you here," she says when I pull my chair up next to her. "I'm glad that you two kids are getting along again."

"Your son is a very wonderful man, ma'am."

"And your husband?" she asks.

The question takes me by surprise. She always came off as so polite and nice that I had forgotten that she's the mother of a child that I have hurt.

"My husband, not so much. I have discovered a number of things that, well, let's just say are less than endearing, most of them are quite illegal and hurtful."

"I see," she says, holding her hands in her lap.

I know that this is not much of an explanation so I continue, "I never married him because I loved him. There was only one person I have ever loved and that is your son."

Henry glances over at his mom and smiles.

"It's true," I say. "I had to marry Franklin to save my parents' company. It's kind of a secret but I hope you guys won't tell anyone."

"I won't," she says. "But I'm a little surprised that you're telling me this."

I shrug. "I don't know," I say. "I guess, I just feel like I can trust you."

"Is that so?" she says with a glint in her eye. "I kind of get the feeling that you think that I'm dying."

I gasp a little, surprised by her candor.

When I look at Henry, he starts to laugh.

"I'm sorry about that, I have kind of a deadpan sense of humor," Mrs. Asher says.

They both laugh and I can't help but join them.

29

HENRY

When my mother closes her eyes to rest, Aurora and I go back to the waiting room to talk. The cafeteria has opened and we buy some breakfast food but the lights in there are too hard, so neither of us want to stay there.

In the waiting room, we sit in the corner and she tucks her feet up to her chest, wrapping her arms around them. I turn my body toward her but I'm too tall and big to ball myself up.

"Thank you so much for coming with me," I say, biting into my danish. I haven't eaten since last night and the explosion of sugar with blueberry marmalade overwhelms my senses. It's the most delicious thing I've ever had.

"Of course," she says.

"No, thank you," I insist. "I know that this was a very dangerous thing for you to do. I know that Franklin watches your every move and this was… I just can't believe that you did this for me."

She shrugs and picks at her croissant.

"I want to be here for you and for your mom. I don't wanna be at home, not ever. That's not my home. He's a stranger and he's someone that hurts me. It's difficult to talk about but every time I'm there, it's like I'm walking on land covered in land mines. One false move and everything is going to blow up."

"I wish that there was something I could do," I say.

"There is. You can just be here for me. You can take all of that evidence that I collected and keep it somewhere very safe. Then you can help me come up with a plan to make him go away, to expose every evil thing that he and all those other people have done."

We talk for a little bit about what Aurora found and about all of those men with underage girls and boys. We talk a lot about the altered video and how involved her father is in this whole thing. Then I bring up the one thing that I have been thinking about for a while now.

"What about your dad?" I ask. "Did you see him on any of those videos?"

"I thought that I might," she admits. "I was really scared to go through them. I really thought that I would see him doing something terrible. I mean, the fake video was one thing but I thought that I might see him hurting someone in a real way. I didn't. I don't think that he was involved. No, I know that he wasn't. At least Franklin doesn't have any evidence of that and I have no idea why he would not keep that video if he had kept videos of the governor and all of those other people."

I let out a sigh of relief. That's some good news. I know that Mr. Tate has done a lot of bad things in his life to get where he is but I'm glad that he has never done that.

I see a crumb in the corner of her lips and I reach over to brush it off. I run my fingers along her lower lip. She tenses it and kisses me. I move my face toward her and press my lips to her mouth.

She tastes like chocolate and home. I bury my fingers in her hair and she runs hers down my neck because finally, in the corner of that waiting room, our world starts to make sense again.

"Uh-hum," someone says, clearing her throat. "Excuse me?"

I pull away from her and see Dr. Kim standing with her chart in front of me.

"I have some good news for you, Henry," she says.

We both stand up and wait.

"Your mother's going to be fine," she says, smiling with her eyes. "Apparently, this has nothing to do with her previous cancer diagnosis. We suspect that this was just a low blood sugar episode mixed with dehydration. She's susceptible to that and we really need to monitor her blood sugar. Otherwise, she can go home."

A wave of relief washes over me and my legs feel weak. I actually take a step back to make sure that I don't drop to the floor.

I look over at Aurora to make sure that I have heard her right and when I see her smile from ear to ear, I know that I haven't imagined it.

Dr. Kim extends her hand but I just wrap my arms around her and give her a big hug.

"Thank you so much," I say over and over again, even though I know that she wants me to stop.

"You're welcome, Henry. I'm really happy for you."

"Come on." Aurora takes my hand and pulls me away from the good doctor. "Let's go see your mom."

30

AURORA

Franklin doesn't ask me much about Ellis and the reason that I have slept over but I know why. I watch the video of what happened in his office the night that I went to the hospital with Henry. The girl doesn't look much older than twelve and he even shows her how to snort cocaine before making her give him a massage.

"This isn't going to happen again," I say to myself.

No matter what, I'm not gonna let another girl get hurt. This is going to end very soon but I decide to give my father another chance to save himself.

That's why I asked my mom to meet me for lunch.

"What are we doing in this godforsaken place?" my mom asks when we walk into the Cheesecake Factory in midtown.

"I need to talk to you somewhere private where no one would follow us," I say.

"Well, we found the right place. I mean, the only people who actually eat here are tourists from flyover states."

I ignore her and try to focus on what I'm here to talk about.

I get right to the point. I tell her what I found and what Dad needs to do.

She looks at me with a blank expression on her face. When the waiter comes around to take her order, she says that she won't be staying long.

"Just a lemonade for me, hon," she says.

"Same," I say. "No ice."

She waits for him to walk away before turning and looking at me.

"Your father had to do what he had to do. You have no right to get involved."

"You knew about this?" I guess.

Leaning over the table, I say, "What were you thinking?"

"We were thinking that we needed that money to save the company."

"You tanked that company stock for no reason."

"Not no reason. That CEO was an asshole and you know it."

I shake my head.

"Besides, self-driving cars? What the hell is that? What are they going to do, stop inventing all of these new robots and machines and give people's jobs back?"

"This isn't about that," I say. "This is a political discussion."

"Everything is a political discussion."

"Dad committed fraud and you know about it; you're involved with it. I'm sure that a lot of federal prosecutors would be very interested to find out exactly what you and that short seller did and how you conspired together to ruin one of the biggest companies in the world."

"We didn't ruin anything," Mom says. "Their stock went down a little bit. We made some money. They have bounced back."

"They wouldn't have to bounce back if this had never happened, but guess what? It did."

Our lemonades come. She takes a sip of hers and pushes it away.

"I don't drink tap water," she says. Grabbing her purse, she gets up from behind the table.

"I have to talk to you." I follow her.

She shakes her head.

"I don't eat at places like this and I don't discuss things that are done and put away. Stop bringing up the past. Stop opening scabs that you have no business touching."

"You have to make Dad go to the FBI," I whisper. "He has got to make a deal."

"Your father is never making any deal with any fucking FBI."

I REALLY THOUGHT that my meeting with my mom would go a lot better, otherwise I wouldn't have even bothered. Still, I don't give up hope on my dad. This is going to happen whether he makes the deal or not but if he does, then at least there's a chance that he won't get as much time.

However we handle Franklin, this is coming to light and my father will have to face the public about his involvement. If he were to go to the authorities with his attorney, then he stands a chance to actually get away with some of it.

No, *getting away* is the wrong way to think about it. He will give them evidence and it will help them build a better case. In return, he will not have to serve a sentence. That's how it works and that's how most people in his position would solve the problem.

Later that afternoon, I find my father in his usual afternoon haunt; an oak covered club where men come to sit around, drink brandy, and talk politics and business like they have for the last couple hundred years. Despite women gaining the ability to vote and own property, we are still not allowed to be members because…tradition or is it misogyny? I keep getting the two confused.

The assistant at the front doesn't want to let me in but he reluctantly goes back and finds my father. When he returns, he shows me down the long hallway and into a dark wooden room with built-in bookshelves going all the way up to the ceiling and even a ladder to make browsing easier. It's a dream come true library for any book fan and it personally reminds me of the one from Beauty and the Beast.

There are two men sitting across from each other, talking in hushed tones. I see my father by the window in a wingback chair, nursing a crystal glass of whiskey.

I expect him to get up and give me a hug but he barely acknowledges my existence. I sit down across from him, pushing my fingers into the velvet of the seat.

"You're not supposed to be here, Aurora. This is my private place."

"I know but I had to talk to you and this can't wait."

He stares icily back into my face.

"I'm at the club," he says, enunciating every syllable.

That's supposed to explain something to me but it goes over my head.

"I have to talk to you—"

"Your mother called me. She told me that you ambushed her and forced her to go to the Cheesecake Factory of all places."

"You make it sound like a war zone," I say.

"Well, I didn't want to do the same thing to you so I thought I would just find you here."

He exhales slowly, laser focusing his gaze on me.

"You need to consider going to the authorities," I say. "You need to talk to a lawyer and try to make this right."

"I'm not making any deals," he says sternly.

He has way too much to lose and he has already sacrificed me, to some degree, to Franklin to save himself and his company.

"Why not?" I ask.

"If I go public with this, if I make a deal, then I'm a dead man. Franklin is the only one protecting me. The guy that I made the deal with, the short seller? He's not your usual white-collar criminal. He's connected. He's got ties and I can't cross him. Why does it matter anyway?"

I want to tell him that Franklin is going down but I force myself to stop.

"Franklin and I are not going to be married for much longer. Your deal with him, I'm not gonna go through with it."

"No, you can't." My father shakes his head. "If you file for divorce or if you pull out, I will no longer have Franklin's protection."

"That's why you have to make a deal," I say.

"No, that's why *you* have to stay married and keep your mouth shut. We made this promise. We're all going to be rich as a result."

"We're already rich, Dad. How much fucking money do you need?"

"We *were* rich, Aurora, but we were upside down on all of our debts and all of our mortgages when I made that deal with Franklin. Why else do you think I promised my only daughter to him? I wouldn't have done it for no good reason. You have to trust me."

I take a deep breath, exhaling ever so slowly. I lick my lips and look out the window.

My mouth is parched.

My lips are cracked. I came here to give him a chance to get out of this but he doesn't believe me.

He doesn't trust me.

What can I do?

"I'm here to help you, Dad. You're not doing me a favor, I'm doing you a favor. Despite everything that you did to me, I'm still sitting here across from you and hoping that you will listen to me and make that deal. That's the best advice that I can offer you."

31

AURORA

L ater that evening, I meet up with Henry at our local bookstore. It's a chain, two floors tall, and plenty of space for waiting, drinking coffee, and just mingling.

It used to be one of my favorite places to go but now it's also my only solace. Franklin is supposed to be working late but I still give him the courtesy of telling him where I am. So far, he has been rather trusting and I hope that continues just for a little bit longer.

Still, I'm cautiously optimistic.

Henry arrives right on time. He meets me in the stacks, on the second floor, near the philosophy section, which is what most people tend to avoid.

He tries to give me a peck on the cheek but I shake my head no.

Instead, when he sits down across from me at the little round table, I reach over and squeeze his hand. He lets it drop to his lap and there, our fingers intertwine and grasp for one another's.

"My mother is feeling a lot better," he says after a few moments. "Thank you so much for being there for me. I don't know how I would've survived it otherwise."

"Of course, I wanted to be there."

"I know and that's why I love you." His fingers wrap around mine again and give me a strong, forceful squeeze.

I tell him what little success that I had talking to my parents and then I tell him about my plan. He listens carefully and doesn't say anything for a long time.

"What do you think?" I ask.

He shakes his head.

"We have to do it. I can't think of another way."

"It's too dangerous. What if..."

"There's no way around it. If I don't stop this, those girls are going to keep coming in there, and they're going to keep getting hurt. Everything will continue just as it has and no one will protect them."

"Can you just go to the police?" he asks. "Maybe they can do something."

"No," I say confidently, even though I am anything but that. "I can't risk them screwing this up. I can't risk their superiors finding out. You have seen all of those men on those videos. The chief of police wasn't there but who knows what he owes and to whom. This is the only way."

Finally, he gives me a slight nod. His fingers make their way up my arm and all the way up to my elbow. He's grasping onto me, holding on, trying desperately to either stop me or be there for me. Maybe both at the same time.

I tap my foot nervously on the floor. I fold the fingers of my other hand into my palm and out again, stretching it out and looking at the whites of my knuckles.

"I have to go to the bathroom," I say after a moment.

I make my way inside and pause near the mirror. Suddenly, a flash of hot heat overwhelms me and turns my chest red. I flip the switch and place my hands underneath the stream of falling water. It's ice cold and it feels amazing when I splash it on my face.

I don't see him until his fingers run down my side. I glance up and our eyes meet in the mirror. He places his lips to my neck and slowly makes his way down to my shoulders.

"Someone's going to come in," I whisper.

He shakes his head no and says, "I locked the door."

He pulls the top of my sweater away, exposing my bra strap and my collarbone. I glance over at the door and see that the lock is indeed turned.

He flips me around and kisses me on the mouth. I kiss him back. A fire between us builds quickly and overwhelms us both. I know that someone could come in at any moment, or rather knock on the door, but that just seems to add to the excitement. I search for his belt and unbuckle it within a few movements. I pull up on his shirt, running my fingers down his chiseled abs.

Henry slides down my leggings and I quickly step out of one foot in order to create space for his body. He props me up onto the counter, rubbing his hard cock on top of my panties. My body yearns for his. I grab onto the sink with my hands as he grabs onto my breasts.

He lifts up my shirt, undoes my bra, and takes one of them in his mouth. I hear a loud latex sound as his slides on the condom. I continue to kiss his mouth as he uses his other hand to slide my panties to one side and thrusts himself inside.

My body is waiting for him. I'm wet and I take him in as far as he can come. With each move, we become more and more like one. My core burns for him. With my arms practically pinned behind my back, in order to hold myself up, he has his way with all of me.

I turn my head back and let him run his tongue all over my neck, my breasts, and up to my mouth. He continues to pierce me over and over again until a wave of pleasure rushes over me.

It comes so quickly; it catches me completely by surprise. I wanted to hold off, I want to enjoy the moment more but it just covers me entirely and my body begins to quiver.

"Let go," he whispers into my ear, pushing himself further in, over and over again.

Whatever tension I felt, whatever worries plagued me only moments before suddenly disappear. They disperse along with all of my fears and second-guesses.

Somewhere in the distance, there's a knock on

the door. They keep trying the knob but I am too far away and lost in my own head, to tell them to get the fuck away.

Instead, I hold onto Henry. I wait for him to get there.

It doesn't take long.

A few more strong movements and suddenly everything is right in the world.

I hold him as he moans my name.

32

HENRY

A couple of days later is my first TV appearance as a crime journalist. Aurora is also there.

She has been making the rounds around various departments with Franklin's encouragement, in an effort to figure out where she can make the most impact.

Today is her third day working with live news.

The anchor that will be interviewing me is named Glenn Reeves. He's popular, well-known, and has the ego of someone with four times his ratings. I met him briefly but I made a deal with the producer of the segment.

He's very good at interviews and prefers to go into these sorts of situations not knowing much. It wouldn't be the way I would approach interviewing someone but I go with the flow.

My purpose here is to report and promote the O.J. Simpson podcast that I've been working on and to hopefully bring over some of the viewers to my show.

As I sit in front of the mirror, a woman about twenty-years older than I am puts on a thick pound of foundation on my face.

I try to get a hold of my nerves.

I've never done something so public before, as I have always been able to hide behind the microphone. Being live and having people actually see me scares the shit out of me but this is the only way to do it.

"How are you feeling?" Glenn asks, popping his head into the dressing room.

I glance at the time to make sure that I'm not running late.

"No, you're good. I was just walking by. I heard about your podcast, great job."

"Thank you, that really means a lot and thank you so much for having me on."

"Hey, where would the network news be if we didn't have an old rating hog to report on like the O.J. Simpson case."

I stare at him, unsure how I should respond.

My heart races but not just because I'm about to be on network television. It's more than that.

"Listen, don't be nervous," Glenn says, with the casual smile that made millions fall in love with him.

In only a minute, he can become your best friend, or at least make it feel like it.

"It's just my first time doing something like this," I say.

"All that is going to happen is that I'll ask you questions and you'll tell me what you found out and what you're working on. It's a ten-minute segment and it'll fly by in thirty seconds. You have nothing to worry about. You're in great hands."

"I appreciate the encouragement." I give him a confident nod and watch him walk away.

If only he knew what is about to happen…

A few minutes later, I stand in the studio and watch Leslie Mountain, the weatherman, predict more doom and gloom in terms of the plummeting temperatures. Everyone else at the desk makes jokes about how much they hate winter while Leslie tries to liven up the mood. I watch them practically blame the snowstorm and the low hanging clouds on him, as if he were the guy creating the situation.

"Listen, it's not like it's my fault." Leslie keeps insisting.

His mouth is still formed into a smile, but with his eyes he is glaring at Glenn and the rest of the morning news team, even scowling a bit.

They cut to the commercial break and one of the female news anchors apologizes to Leslie.

"I'm just getting really sick of this shit," he says. "You all act like it's my fault that the goddamn weather is what it is."

She tries to walk after him, but he rushes away before she can catch up to him.

"So, what do you think about the studio?" Franklin asks, putting his hand on my shoulder.

I flinch. I stop breathing mid-inhale. He is supposed to be upstairs. This isn't going to plan.

"I am... Good. I mean, it's great," I mumble

"I can see that you're not nervous at all," Franklin says sarcastically.

I shrug and try to get a hold of myself. I take a deep breath, shifting my weight from one side to the other.

"Well, you know me, I've never done something like this before. I don't know how I'll be...in front of the camera."

"Oh, don't worry about it," Franklin says. "If those four idiots can do it, anyone can."

He is right beside my ear, just out of shot but his condescension is not lost on the on-air team.

Back in the makeup room, I heard a conversation about just how much they hate him and dislike the fact that he bought Tate Media.

"Besides," Franklin continues, "this is gonna be really great exposure for you and for the podcast. People love those true crime shows, right?"

I nod and shift my weight again, stepping slowly from one side to the other.

"Hell, the Discovery Channel started a whole separate channel devoted exclusively just to their true crime stories."

"Is that what you're thinking of doing?" I ask.

"True crime is cheap to produce and the best part is that you can keep talking about those old cases and people keep watching. O.J. Simpson, Scott Peterson, Robert Blake. All of those stories are brand new to younger viewers and it provides an element of nostalgia to the older ones. They remember when that story was all over the news and now, they can get a nice processed version about what *really* happened."

"I hope that your cynicism doesn't rub off on me anytime soon," I say.

Franklin's eyes focus on mine, and then he starts to laugh. I've never seen him laugh this hard. It builds somewhere deep in his stomach and comes out in waves, one stronger than the next.

"I didn't think that that was particularly funny," I point out.

"I like you, Henry. You're not much of a yes-man or ass licker and you'd be surprised how unique that is in this business."

Maybe that makes me an idiot.

When has standing up to your boss ever gotten you anything positive in life?

That shit only works on television. In real life, that's the kind of thing that will get you fired and blacklisted from good career opportunities.

33

HENRY

F ranklin showing up down here, in the studio, is against the plan. I already have certain reservations about what is going to happen and whether this is the best approach but now I feel completely uncertain.

I take a few deep breaths to calm my nerves but my heart continues to pound from the inside out.

One of the producers walks me to my seat. The commercial break is almost over.

Now, it's just the two of us, Glenn and me. All of the other personalities are standing in the wings, with their heads buried in their phones.

No one is expecting the segment to be anything but a simple promotion for my O.J. Simpson podcast.

"Take a deep breath, man. It's going to be all right," Glenn says.

I know that my nervousness is showing.

That's bad.

I grab my thigh underneath the table and rub my fingers on it.

Calm down, calm the fuck down, I say silently to myself over and over again.

I glance over to the television cameras. Aurora is standing next to the table with all of the food, near the office. She takes a step closer to me. Her arms are crossed in front of her chest and her eyes are laser-focused on mine.

She gives me a nod.

I shake my head no.

I want to ask her, what if we wait?

What if right now is *not* the best time?

But I can't.

All I can do is move my head slightly in Franklin's direction and watch her react.

She gives me another nod.

She knows that he's here and she wants to stick to the plan.

Okay, I take a deep breath. It's showtime.

Someone counts down and the red light comes on. Words start to scroll up the teleprompter, and

Glenn introduces me with the ease and expertise of a veteran newscaster.

"So, Henry, over the years, the O.J. Simpson case has been covered extensively," Glenn says, turning away from the teleprompter. "Why don't I ask you a question that all of my viewers are thinking right now?"

I laugh. "Sure."

Out of the corner of my eye, I look over at Aurora. I don't see her by the catering table. She must be in the control room. I have an earphone that the producers have given me, but I'm also wearing another secret one.

"Go ahead," Aurora says into my ear. "I'm ready."

"What would that be?" I ask Glenn.

"Well, have there really been any great new developments in that case? I mean, why do this?"

I swallow hard.

It's the moment of truth.

I lean back against the chair and turn a little bit more toward the audience, still keeping my eyes on Glenn.

"Actually, I have a little bit of a surprise. I have been working on another story, undercover, so to speak. This is as good a time as any to bring it all to light."

"New story?" Glenn asks.

His demeanor changes. He's no longer his usual soft, cuddly, and confident self.

Instead, I feel his nervousness rise up to the surface.

I look into the audience of producers and cameramen and out of the corner of my eye, I see Franklin.

His head is buried in his phone. After a moment, he looks up, glaring at me.

I turn to Glenn and say, "I have been working on a story about powerful men coercing and sexually assaulting underage girls. I have videos of all of these incidences, recorded by surveillance cameras inside the home of the owner of this network, Franklin Parks."

The studio gets so quiet that you could hear a pin drop. As I tell him about everything that Aurora has found, I watch Franklin rush over to the control room to stop the broadcast.

But Aurora is too fast. She locks the doors and he's left pounding on the glass from the outside.

"Franklin Parks has orchestrated the systematic abuse of multiple underage girls from underprivileged backgrounds. I have proof of all of these men coming in and abusing these girls under his roof. Let me show you what I'm talking about."

I point Glenn's attention to the monitor in front of us and watch the first video of the governor of New Jersey and the girl with the blacked-out face in Franklin's massage room.

Big portions of it are, of course, cut to protect the innocent. Most of the content is too graphic to show on the morning news but Jackie has edited enough of them together to show the face of the governor, the attorney general, the senator from New York, and a few other higher-ups that regular people would recognize.

"This is hard to believe," Glenn says, shaking his head. "But at the same time, the videos… How did you get these?"

"I have a source and he or she is willing to come forward at the right time and place. Given the power of the people that are involved in the crime, I decided that the best way to expose the truth is to show the American people directly."

I'm about to say something else but before I know it, Franklin jumps on stage and punches me in the face. Blood gushes into my mouth and I make a fist and swing at him. I make contact and he falls to the floor. I punch him again and again. When I take a breath, he raises his hand and knocks the wind out of me.

I pause for a moment to try to catch my breath and when I look around all I see are phones pointing in my face.

Everyone is recording everything.

"How could you do this to me?" Franklin whines and punches me again in the ear.

My head starts to buzz and I lose my footing.

"How could you do this to *them*?" I bark back, bashing him in his chin. He falls down again, this time without getting up.

Aurora rushes out of the control room and grabs onto my hand. I look down at my knuckles. The skin has been torn off and they're bleeding profusely.

Being the professional that he is, Glenn doesn't stop reporting. It's almost as if having a real story right before him, unfolding right here in the studio, invigorates him. Instead of trying to cut to a commercial to protect the station, he grabs the microphone and walks right to me.

"Henry Asher," he asks, "can you tell me what just happened? How are you feeling? How did you feel having your boss, the CEO of this company, jump right out here on stage and punch you on live television, in front of all of America?"

"Well, I was a little bit surprised," I say, still trying to catch my breath. I take a few forceful breaths and add, "Perhaps I shouldn't be. We have exposed his lies and his secrets and now everyone knows who he really is."

Franklin doesn't get another chance to hit me.

The FBI are already here. They have been waiting in the wings and they put him in handcuffs right in front of all of the cameras.

That was the deal. They promised Aurora that they wouldn't arrest him until the live broadcast.

It took her some time to convince them. They weren't sure it was such a good idea but she promised them that he would incriminate himself.

She was right.

34

HENRY

After they arrest Franklin, Aurora follows me to the makeup room and applies ice to my face.

Neither of us know what to say for a while. This is only the beginning of the story. She checks her phone and scrolls through Twitter.

Stories and comments start to appear like an avalanche. The first story to hit, the one that Franklin saw on his phone before he tried to break into the control room, was written by me for Tate News, an online magazine owned by Tate Media that Aurora arranged placement for.

I spent all night last night writing up all the details, quoting and verifying sources when I could. The story is developing and ongoing.

Aurora is not the only eyewitness as there were other employees who have seen things but have been forced to sign nondisclosure agreements to keep quiet. When I told them about the tapes, they finally decided to come forward.

At first, I was categorically against Aurora's plan. I wasn't sure that we would be able to pull it off.

So many things had to go right.

I had to write the right story. The story had to be published. Besides the fact that it also had to be fact checked by the editor.

Nothing was set in stone.

We had agreed on the date and everyone promised to keep their word to not disclose it until it was published, but that was just one part one of the plan.

Aurora wanted to expose Franklin on television. Live.

We had no idea what kind of relationship he had with his anchors or the producers of the morning show so we couldn't let any of them in on what I was about to do.

So, we hatched the plan that I would come on the show to promote my podcast. Franklin had arranged the whole thing, but little did he know that the story would actually be about him.

When he found out, he tried to get into the control room and stop it from happening but Aurora was already there. She had locked the doors and she told them to keep rolling. The more I talked, the more the executive producer believed us.

So, when she put in the cut-up video files to broadcast for everyone to see, Franklin couldn't stop her.

None of this was a given or certainty.

There was a lot of luck involved.

The one thing that I did not expect him to do was to rush the stage but that just added to the sizzle of the story. After that, social media took over and it blew up.

"How is this?" Aurora asks, pressing the ice to my eye.

"It's fine," I say, pushing it away.

In reality, the ice is more painful than the bruise.

Aurora continues to scroll through her phone, checking Twitter and Facebook and the stories directly on Google News.

"What's going on?" I ask.

"The news outlets seem to be picking it up. It's definitely trending. More and more people are retweeting and talking about it. Your article has a thousand comments already."

I lie back in the chair and smile.

"Okay," I say quietly to myself.

I did something good. I don't know what's going to happen from here but at least I did my part.

"Everything is going to work out, right?" Aurora asks, taking my hand in hers.

I snap out of the trance and look into her big, wide eyes. Suddenly, I remember that she had to do a lot more to get here than I did.

I wrote the article, I told the world what was going on, but it was she who did all the dirty work.

If she didn't get those recordings, if she didn't risk her life, and if she didn't let him hurt her, to some degree, none of this would've happened.

The FBI assured me that they were going to press charges. We gave them a lot of evidence. There's still a lot to go through but it has to work out.

Aurora shakes her head, clenching and unclenching her jaw.

"What's wrong?" I ask.

"I don't know," she says with tears welling up in her eyes. "I want to be happy and I want to celebrate but I just have this heavy heart. What if we haven't done enough?"

There's a knock at the door and Agent Richter walks in. I've only talked to him once before, when I came into his office and told him about our plan.

Then I invited him to the studio to watch the show unfold in real time. I wasn't sure if he was going to show up. Frankly, I wasn't sure if he even believed me.

He walks over to me and shakes my hand.

Then he does the same thing to Aurora.

"We have a lot of evidence to go through and we do not like to go public before we have all of our ducks in a row but Henry told me that that was the only way you were going to do it. In either case, I appreciate all the investigative work you two have done. We're going to do our best to make those assholes pay for it."

We talk a little bit more about the details of the legal process to come but when I see Aurora's eyes glazing over and the tiredness that has built up from the last few months catching up with her, I cut the conversation short.

"This has been quite a stressful day for us, Agent Richter. I hope you don't mind but we would like to go home, get some rest, and regroup. If you need us for anything, we are always available."

"That's a very good idea, son," he says.

After watching him walk out of the room, I reach over and grab Aurora's hand. I interlace my fingers with hers and squeeze tightly.

35

HENRY

The next two weeks are a blur. We spend most of them in bed and the rest talking to authorities and giving statements. Everyone wants to hear everything firsthand.

That's okay.

We want to tell the story. The world deserves to know. There are, of course, hundreds of opposing articles written by Franklin's people and the defenders of all of those powerful men that went down with him but that doesn't stop us.

Whoever believes us, believes us. We try to control the narrative as much as we can by saying yes to as many interviews as possible but at some point, it all becomes too much.

Then, we get the bad news.

"Franklin has made bail," Aurora says, rushing over to me with her phone.

We stare at the screen.

I don't believe the headline.

Aurora doesn't either. She goes to Google News and scrolls through ten others that say basically the same thing.

"How could they let him out?" she asks. "Don't they know *who he is*?"

I shake my head. "I guess that's the point of the trial." I want to say but I know better.

Franklin Parks got out because he had the money and the power to get out. He hired the right lawyers and they made the right deals.

Besides, what did we expect? That the most powerful man running the most powerful media company in the world is actually going to waste away in prison awaiting trial?

"I need to go there," Aurora says. "He's getting out this afternoon and I want to be there."

"I don't think that's such a good idea," I say.

She shakes her head no and says, "I don't care."

"Why?" I ask. "Why do you want to be there?"

"I don't know, I just feel like I have to. I want to make sure that this is actually happening."

WE BOTH KNOW that this is a terrible idea but we both go anyway.

When we get to the courthouse, there are reporters and onlookers surrounding the place. The police have roped off parts of it but this is public property and everyone is entitled to be here.

Aurora pushes her way to the front and stands right behind the rope.

"You shouldn't be here," I whisper, but she ignores me.

She's wearing a hoodie and dark sunglasses and I hope that none of the reporters will recognize her.

So far, so good.

"Let's stay a little bit in the back." I try to urge her and pull her away but she just nudges my hand off her shoulder.

"I have to be here. I have to see him walk out," Aurora says.

"Please don't do anything," I plead. I have a feeling that something terrible is about to happen.

She shakes her head.

"He's not worth it. I don't want this to be any worse for you."

But she ignores me. I wait beside her with a

cloud of impending doom around me. I can't predict the future but I know that we shouldn't be here. I need to save her. I need to take her away, but she refuses to budge.

Time passes slowly. The next ten minutes feel like an hour.

Finally, the doors open and Franklin comes out surrounded by his army of attorneys.

He makes a brief statement at the top of the steps but then he breaks away and starts to walk down. I glance over at Aurora and watch her eyes laser-focused on him.

She clenches her jaw. Her hands are buried in the pockets of her hoodie but I can see that they are formed into fists. My head starts to pound along with my heart.

What is she going to do?

How can I stop her?

If she runs out and attacks him…the story will become all about her.

There are cameras and phones everywhere. If she were to do anything to him, even look at him funny, it will only diminish her credibility as a witness later on.

I put my hand on the small of her back, but she shrugs me off.

I steady myself for whatever is to come. If she makes a move, I'll stop her.

"Please don't do anything," I whisper into her ear over and over again. "If you do, this whole thing will become about you. And it's about *him*."

"I'm not going to do anything," she says. "I just want to see the son-of-a-bitch."

But I don't believe her.

Franklin walks down a few steps, holding his head up high. I'm staring right at him, and suddenly our eyes meet. He follows my gaze toward Aurora and gives her small, arrogant little smile that says, 'See, I told you. No one's going to believe a word you say and I'm gonna get away with everything.'

I don't take the bait and watch Aurora to make sure she doesn't either. I tense every muscle in my body, prepared to stop her if she were to even make a flinch in his direction.

Suddenly, the sound of a car backfiring startles me.

A moment later, I realize that it's a gunshot.

Two more follow.

I grab Aurora and cover her body with my own. I feel her breathing underneath me and hear the beating of my own heart in between my ears.

When I look up, I see Franklin lying on the steps and three puddles of blood growing wider and wider over the steps below him.

EPILOGUE

AURORA

When I told Henry that I wanted to go to the courthouse to see Franklin, he was worried that I was going to be the one to attack him. What he didn't expect was that there are other people who have been hurt a lot worse than I have.

What none of us who stood on those white steps knew was the pain of the father who tried to avenge his daughter. The girl was sexually assaulted and raped by my husband and his friends, all prominent men with private planes to their names. Franklin had recorded this scene as well, and the FBI found it on another computer at another one of his homes.

Franklin Parks did not survive the attack. He

died on the scene and I wasn't even a little bit sorry for that.

Afterward, through a lot of paperwork and with the help of many attorneys, Tate Media became mine.

My father had transferred the majority stakeholder position to Franklin shortly before he was arrested and after his death, I had inherited it along with all of the other properties that he had to his name.

Once the company was mine, I put back all of the money that my father stole from the employees' pension funds by selling three of my parents' houses and the majority of their other real estate holdings. The company is barely solvent but with a lot of hard work and additional product lines, I know that I can get it back to profitability.

The trials of the men involved who appeared in Franklin's video collection are all ongoing. Only two have pled guilty in exchange for reduced sentences and others are fighting their charges. It will be years before the victims get any justice but at least everything those evil men have done is out in the open. For that I am thankful.

My father waited a long time to make a deal with the FBI regarding the fraud that he'd perpetuated against Tate Media. He is serving a seven-year sentence. His partner in the video hoax and the fraud got ten years. I don't know if my father's life is still in danger because I'm currently taking a long hiatus from communicating with my parents. Instead, I'm trying to figure out my own role in this world.

I MEET with Henry for lunch at our favorite diner not far away from work. He has been nominated for the Pulitzer Prize as a result of the investigative research that he had done for this case and for the stories that he has published.

"It's so nice to see you," he says. "How's everything?"

I work ten floors up from him and we rarely see each other during the day.

"What are you doing Friday night?" he asks.

I shrug. "No plans."

"Mom wants to have us over for dinner. She has some news."

My throat closes up. No, not again. My mind immediately goes to the worst possible place; the cancer is back.

"No," Henry says, reaching over and squeezing my hand. "This has nothing to do with that. She's fine. Remember, the doctor said that she won't have to come in for a checkup for another six months."

"Okay, good," I say, letting out a sigh of relief. "You just never know, right? I mean, it's like pins and needles with the checkups."

We're in the back booth and he leans over and kisses me.

"What was that?" I ask.

"Just for being so wonderful," he says.

"I just love your mom and I hope she's okay," I say. "Given how I grew up, I had no idea that there were actually nice moms out there."

"Still, it makes me happy," he says, bringing my hand to his lips.

"So, why are we going to Montauk?"

"Apparently, she has a new boyfriend. He's a high school history teacher and they're in love. Her words, not mine."

I laugh. "Your mom deserves to be happy."

"I know, but I still have to grill him. I wouldn't be a good son if I didn't do that."

I stare into his eyes for a long time, feeling utterly at peace. I've never felt this way before. It's like, I don't have a worry in the world because I know that he will always be there for me.

"I love you," I whisper, intertwining his fingers with my own.

"I love you, too," Henry says, leaning over the table and kissing me on the mouth. "I will always love you. Forever. Until the end of time."

I HOPE you enjoyed the Wedlocked Trilogy! Can't get enough of my books? I have a new hate-love, enemies-to-lovers romance full of angst, twists and turns, steamy scenes and second chances. **One-click NOT INTO YOU now!**

I hate you.

I hate your swagger and your attitude.

Once, you were everything that I wanted. After you left, I lost everything.

But then you waltzed back into my life: confident, cocky, and as dark and as beautiful as ever.

You never cheated and you never lied, but that doesn't mean that what you did didn't hurt.

My hatred for you is a fire, you'll never extinguish.

You know this and you take my hand anyway. I want to push you away, but you won't let me.

What happens when I start to cave?

What happens when all of my rage becomes the opposite of hate?

One-click NOT INTO YOU now!

** NOT INTO YOU is the first book of the bestselling author Charlotte Byrd's enemies-to-lovers DUET that will leave you head spinning.

It was previously published as One Semester but the text has been substantially expanded and revised.

Chapter 1

I walk into my dorm room for the first time and take a deep breath. This is the beginning of something new. Something special. All through high school, I felt like college was going to be some sort of epilogue in the chapters of my life. It was everything I worked for, everything I tried so hard to achieve. While everyone else was hanging out, drinking, and going to parties, I kept my nose in my books. But when this day finally arrived, it no longer felt like an epilogue. No, this is a prologue. The beginning of something special.

"What a large room!" my mom exclaims, looking around my new home. The room is quite spacious. However, it's not quite like the walls college students have on television and in movies. The ceiling is pretty high, but the walls are made of painted cinderblocks. White. Barren. So unlike the cozy, light pink room that I have back home.

I walk over to the window. It's a beautiful late August day. I'm on the 16th floor, and from here I can see into other people's apartments across the street.

"I just can't believe that I'm here." I turn around with a puddle of tears stacking up on the bottom of my eyelids. "In New York."

"Oh, sweetie." My mom puts her arms around me. She knows this has been my dream since I was in middle school. Mom gives me a quick hug and looks out of the window with me.

"I just don't know how people live here. It's so crammed!"

I smile. My mom is not a fan of New York. I grew up in Calabasas, a town just north of Los Angeles, where the sky is almost always cloudless and blue and the temperature never gets cooler than seventy degrees Fahrenheit. My family's upper middle class, but not what's considered rich. At least not by LA standards. Still, our family of five lived comfortably in a 3,000 square foot house with a 6,000 square foot yard and a pool.

"I hope you have nice roommates," Mom says.

"Of course she will," Dad pipes in. He's standing in the doorway, clearly not impressed. "I just can't believe that this room costs $17,000 a year! And you have three other roommates."

Mom and I laugh it off. Even though my dad isn't cheap, he always likes to complain about how much things cost.

"Suite mates," I correct him. "I have one roommate and three suite mates." Our rooms are separated by a living room with a little kitchen and there's only one bathroom for everyone to share.

"The room would be just as big if I'd gone to USC and the school would've cost just as much," I add. University of Southern California is both of my parents' alma mater. That's where they met thirty years ago.

"Yeah, at least you would've been closer to home and wouldn't need a plane ticket to come see us." He shrugs. I roll my eyes. We've been over this thousands of times before. Now, they joke about it more than anything else. They both know that Columbia has been my dream school for as long as I could remember. And when I got my acceptance packet, I think pretty much everyone knew that that's where I was headed.

"I'd just like to see you when it gets into the 20s and 30s here and you have class at 8 a.m.," Mom says. "It's not always this nice out from what I hear."

"I was fine in Colorado," I say. Except that I'm terrified of the cold. I can't wait for the changing leaves and the beautiful crisp fall, but the long hard winter? I don't know.

Both of my parents laugh. "A few week-long skiing trips hardly qualify as experience. Besides, Winter Park is a small, sunny town. A six-month winter in New York where everything gets slushy and the snow is black from the cars and the pollution is something else entirely," Mom says.

I nod.

"I think I'll manage," I say, putting on a brave face. I turn away from the window to change the topic.

"So which bed do you think I should choose?" The room has two of everything. Two beds. Two standing wardrobes. Two desks. Two chairs. Two windows. One looking out on 116th Street. One looking out onto Broadway.

"If you take this one onto 116th Street, it should be a little quieter," Mom says just as an ambulance turns on its siren and rushes down the street. "Or maybe not."

I decide on that one anyway.

"If you two are done staring at the blank room, I think it's about time to go back downstairs and get more of your stuff, young lady," Dad says, glued to his cell phone.

My mom and dad are both doctors, but they recently started a clinical trials consulting firm, which has made them busier than they've ever been when they were in practice.

"I'll be right down," I say. "I'm just going to put some of these things away."

Right after Mom and Dad leave, the door swings open and a tall, voluptuous brunette walks in.

"Alice?" she asks. Her whole face lights up, putting me at ease.

"Doreen?" I ask.

"Oh, no, no, no." She shakes her head. I extend my hand, but she pulls me into a warm hug instead. "Call me Juliet, *please*. I hate Doreen."

"Okay." I nod. Coming from LA, I'm well familiar with name changes. Three girls at my school changed their names officially before they got their boob jobs before graduation.

"Oh my God, you're so cute!" She laughs. "And little. You're from LA, right? You have to tell me your secret. Agh, why am I still holding this?"

She drops her bags onto her bed and leans the long mirror she's carrying against the wall. "I thought we'd hang this on the door."

Aha! I finally realize it. That's what's weird about this room; there are no mirrors.

"Great idea. I completely forgot to bring a lengthwise mirror," I say. "Actually, I thought there would be one here."

At home, I have three in my room. I help Juliet hang the mirror on the back of our door and try to see if it still closes. It swings along with the door, but we're just going to be careful.

"So?" Juliet turns to me. "What's your secret?"

"Secret?"

"In staying so small. I know you LA girls have your ways."

I smile. I look at myself in the mirror. Skinny jeans, size one, flip-flops, white t-shirt. No bra. 32A breasts. Long scraggly blonde hair. Hardly any makeup. Next to Juliet, I look like a child. She tosses her dark curls over her head to give them more volume and reapplies her bright red lipstick. She's wearing fake lashes and every part of her face is contoured, giving her beautiful highlights across her forehead and bringing out her cheekbones.

"No secret, really." I shrug. I've had plenty of my own issues with weight.

"Agh, if you say eat healthy and exercise, I'm going to throw up."

"You definitely don't hold back, do you?" I smile.

"No, babe. I call it like I see it. Hope that's okay."

I nod. "More than okay." I welcome her honesty. It's a breath of fresh air after LA where everyone is nice. But too nice. No one says a bad thing to your face. Not even when you really need to hear it.

"Mainly, I try not to eat carbs at night. Avoid processed foods. My mom buys only organic and farmers market food. Not too much dairy. Lean proteins and fish. Stuff like that."

"That explains it." She tosses her hair again. "So no burgers with chili cheese fries?"

I shake my head. "No, not really."

I shudder at the thought, actually. I may be thin here, but back home, girls from my class were much smaller. I'm what they called big-boned.

"That's more like guy food, isn't it?" I ask.

"Not when it's twenty degrees out and you're coming back from the bar at 4 a.m. Those spicy fries will really warm you up from the inside out."

Again with the cold. Before it scares me even more, I decide that it's time for me to go help my parents with the rest of my bags.

My phone beeps.

WHERE ARE YOU? Dad texts.

"I'VE GOTTA GO," I say. "Need to get the rest of my stuff from downstairs. Are you going to stick around? But my parents are here. I'd love for you to meet."

"Yes, definitely!" Juliet smiles and tosses her hair again. Apparently, hair can never have enough volume.

Chapter 2

. . .

I WALK OUT into our living room. The accommodations here are a bit more furnished: an ugly blue couch that desperately needs a throw or a few pillows to make it look at least mildly presentable and two identical green recliners that look like they came from some third-rate thrift store. Is there actually a store that manufactures these ugly things? A halfway acceptable coffee table, which has a French country distressed look, except that it's not cute. It looks like it was actually distressed by the passage of time, not a carefully planned painting job. And a few end tables, which are mismatched in both color and height. Everything in this living room is wrong. And yet, everything about this place feels so right!

My palms grow sweaty from the excitement. I'm actually in New York.

N-e-w Y-o-r-k!!!

I feel like I'm in some fabulous movie, about to embark on the adventure of my life. I'm ready to put on a fabulous pair of fall boots, black tights, and a little black skirt and walk around Central Park with a latte like a real New Yorker!

"Alice?" His voice pierces my fantasy. I know

who it is before I turn around. It's a voice I could never forget no matter how I try.

"Alice? Is that you?" He grabs my arm, turning me around.

"Hudson? What're you doing here?" I ask.

"What're *you* doing here?" he asks.

We stand, staring at each other for a moment. He hasn't changed. Not much. But there wasn't much time for him to change. It has only been two weeks since our infamous breakup. Still, he looks more grown up. His light brown hair is shorter now. He's dressed in a nice pair of slim cut jeans, which accentuates his ass, and his favorite light blue t-shirt with an outline of a penguin on the front. He's as tan as he always was; that's what happens when you surf every day of the summer, no matter what. But his eyes are bluer than they used to be. Maybe it's the light. Or the distance.

"Alice, can you help me-" Juliet comes out of our room. "Well, hello there. I'm Juliet," she says flirtatiously.

"Hi, I'm Hudson Hilton," he says, extending his hand. "I'm your new suite mate."

"Oh, sweet! I didn't know this place was co-ed. Did you, Alice?"

No, I didn't know either. I also didn't know that

it was possible to be assigned to the same suite as your fuckin' ex-boyfriend. And not just some ex-boyfriend, the one who broke your heart into a million tiny pieces.

"Man, you're quite tan, isn't he, Alice?"

"I'm from California." He shrugs.

"Ah, that explains it! Alice is from California, too."

"Yes, I know." He nods. "We actually know each other."

Juliet jumps back in surprise as if this news means as much to her as it means to me.

"You went to the same high school?" she asks.

"What're you doing here, Hudson?" I ask.

"Listen, this is some sort of accident, okay? I didn't mean for this to happen. I didn't even know this suite was co-ed. I was assigned here. Just like you."

"Well, I can't stay here if you're going to be here," I say.

"What?! Why?" Juliet throws her arm around me. "No, you can't leave, sweetie. Who knows what kind of crazy girl I'm going to have to room with next."

I shake my head. I can't deal with this. I can't even be in the same room as him!

"Hudson?" I hear my mom's voice from somewhere behind me. "What're you doing here, Hudson?"

"Hello, Dr. Summers. Dr. Summers." Hudson gives both my parents a brief hug. My dad is actually so surprised to see him that he manages to look away from his phone.

"It looks like Alice and I have been assigned to the same suite." He shrugs.

"Mom, I have to go talk to someone about moving. I can't stay here. Live with him."

"Alice, don't be rude," she whispers to me and then turns back to Hudson. "How's your mom and dad, Hudson? Are they here?"

"They're in New York, but they had some errands to run. We're meeting up for dinner later, after I unpack and stuff. I think they're going to come see the place then."

"Oh, that's nice. Well, send them our best." My mom smiles. She knows almost everything that happened between us, but she's still polite and courteous. In this moment, I both love her and hate her.

"Excuse me, I've got to unpack," I say and walk back into my room. I sit on the bed and try to assess the situation.

"What's wrong?" Juliet bursts into the room only a few seconds later, followed by my mom.

I shake my head. I can't talk.

"Juliet, is it?" my mom says. "I'm Dr. Summers."

"Yes, of course. I'm so sorry."

"It's okay. Are you okay, Alice?" my mom asks.

"I'd love to give you a few moments, Dr. Summers. But I just can't leave without knowing what's going on here. You know Hudson from before, don't you?"

"He's her high school boyfriend," Mom explains. "They dated for two years. Long distance over this past year. And they broke up a few weeks ago."

"Oh. My. God."

"Well, actually, Hudson broke up with Alice. Very suddenly," my mom adds.

"Shut up!" Juliet exclaims. "What an asshole!"

"Yes, he is a bit of an asshole," Mom whispers.

Juliet goes on a rant about how much men suck and how much it sucks that we need them. I don't really agree, but I agree in this moment. I like how protective she already is of me. But I still can't stay here.

"I have to go talk to someone in housing," I finally say, getting off the bed.

"Oh, sweetie." My mom shakes her head. "Are you sure?"

"What should I do instead? Just stay here and live with him all semester?"

My mom sighs. "I don't know. But if that's what you want…"

"No, you can't. Alice, please! You can't leave me alone with that asshole, if he is really an asshole."

"He's not really an asshole, Juliet. He's a nice guy. I just can't live with him. That's all."

Chapter 3

WHEN I WALK OUT of the room, I find my father and Hudson discussing the biomedical stocks together. Hudson's planning on majoring in Economics and has already invested a substantial amount of his grandparents' birthday gifts into a few high performing and promising funds. My dad is always on the lookout for stock tips and never passes an opportunity to get one, even if it's from the guy who broke his daughter's heart. On the other hand, what the hell do I expect him to do? Ignore him like a child? It's not like he cheated on me. Or hit me. Or anything unforgivable. He just broke up with me.

Definitely. Can't. Stay. Here.

"Where are you going, Alice?" my dad asks as I try to sneak my way past them.

"Housing," I say without turning around.

"Alice, c'mon. You don't have to do this!" Hudson yells after me.

"Maybe I should go after her?" I hear him ask my dad.

"No, it's better to just let her go, son." My dad stops him, to my great relief. A knot forms in the back of my throat. Tears are about to start flowing. Luckily, the elevator doors close before anyone sees me crying.

"You're going to be okay, Alice." My mom holds me on the way downstairs. I try to wipe away some tears when the elevator stops at different floors and more people get in.

"Oh, don't worry, honey. It's just first day jitters. You're going to be just fine." A helpful woman about my mom's age pats me on the back of my head.

"I'm here dropping off my third one and it

never gets any easier, does it?" she asks, turning to my mother.

Mom shakes her head.

"I've done this twice already, but this is the first one that went so far," she says and goes on to talk about what it was like to take my older sisters to college. Stephanie went to USC and Jacqueline went to UC Berkeley.

I dry my tears and wait for the elevator to finally get downstairs. The process takes forever as kids are moving in and out and the elevator has to stop at practically every floor. On top of all that, my mom makes a new friend at every stop.

By the time we reach the ground floor, I can't control the flow of tears any longer. It has only been two weeks since Hudson dumped me over an arduous six-hour conversation. I'm not anywhere close to getting over him. He has been in my life for the last two years of high school. He has been my love for way longer than that. No, I can't even think about this now. Not if I don't want my eyes to puff up to the size of tomatoes and me to be walking around like some sorry homesick kid the rest of the day.

"It's going to be fine," I say to Mom as we exit the building. The humidity outside envelops us in a thick blanket. It's so thick that I can practically taste the water as we walk through it.

"Of course you are." Mom takes my hand. Many kids are embarrassed of their parents, but I've never been. Until this moment, that is. I suddenly become keenly aware of the fact that I'm crying and holding my mom's hand on the first day of school. I drop her hand immediately. She either doesn't notice or doesn't make a fuss.

The block is overflowing with humanity. There are wide-eyed college freshmen flooding both sidewalks and spilling out onto the streets. Their proud parents are double parked in their cars, helping their kids unpack their bags and thousands of other Bed Bath & Beyond products into large containers on wheels.

At the Housing office, a long line of eager and tired freshmen wraps the outside of the building. We wait in silence for close to an hour until it's finally our turn.

A freckled, tired girl with a tight bun greets us with a lackluster enthusiasm.

"How can I help you?" she asks, barely looking up. Her name tag says Tina.

"Hi, Tina. My daughter has been assigned to a suite with her ex-boyfriend. The whole situation is very complicated and she can't possibly stay there."

"Okay, let me see what I can do." Tina asks for my name and ID. I still don't have my student ID, so I hand her my license. She types and scrolls and hums and then types again. Mom and I just wait.

"No, I'm sorry. We don't have anywhere else to relocate you."

"What?!" I don't believe it. "How can that be? Are you sure?"

"Yes, every dorm is filled." Tina shrugs. She clearly doesn't understand the direness of this situation.

"But you don't understand. I can't live there! He's my ex-boyfriend. It was a bad breakup. I can't see him again. Not every day!"

Suddenly, something I said gets Tina's attention. "Do you have a restraining order against him?"

"Restraining order? Why would I have a restraining order?"

"Was he abusive?" Tina clarifies. But she's still talking in Sanskrit.

"Abusive? No, of course not."

"Well, then there's nothing we can do. You two were matched according to our compatibility algorithm. Those things are typically pretty accurate."

"Well, of course they were compatible." Mom steps in. "That's why they dated for two years. But they've broken up. You can't really expect my daughter to live with her ex-boyfriend for a whole year?"

"There's no need to get an attitude, ma'am," Tina says sternly. "And no, I don't expect her to live there for a year. Just one semester. In November, you can apply again and get reassigned. So that will be only four months."

"I can't live with him for one semester!"

"Alice, there's a lot of people waiting. That's your only option. Unless your mom wants to rent you some crappy, bed-bug infested studio apartment on Amsterdam for $1500 a month."

Before I can reply, the guy waiting behind me in line pushes his way past me to the counter and starts complaining to Tina about the size of his mattress.

I look at my mom. She shrugs. Defeated, we head toward the exit.

A big part of me wants to stomp my feet and insist on that studio on Amsterdam. Maybe if I make it a big enough deal then my parents would cave. But $1500 a month is way more than the dorm. And after casually looking around Craigslist the week before, I know that Tina's not much off on that price or the quality of the possible places.

"So what do you want to do?" Mom asks.

"I want to get a latte and go to sleep. Then I want to wake up and find out this was all just some bad dream."

She hugs me. I don't pull away. She smells of Chanel No. 5, as always, her favorite perfume, and it reminds me of home.

"Daddy will be really happy if you suddenly decide to transfer to USC," she whispers.

"I know. But I won't be." I smile. "Okay. Okay. Enough with the pity party."

I pull away from her.

"It's just one semester, right? One semester. I can do that. I think. How bad could it be?"

Can't wait to read more? **One-click NOT INTO YOU now!**

CONNECT WITH CHARLOTTE BYRD

Sign up for my **newsletter** to find out when I have new books!

You can also join my Facebook group, **Charlotte Byrd's Reader Club**, for exclusive giveaways and sneak peaks of future books.

I appreciate you sharing my books and telling your friends about them. Reviews help readers find my books! Please leave a review on your favorite site.

Sign up for my newsletter: https://www. subscribepage.com/byrdVIPList

Join my Facebook Group: https://www.facebook. com/groups/276340079439433/

Bonus Points: Follow me on BookBub and Goodreads!

ALSO BY CHARLOTTE BYRD

All books are available at ALL major retailers! If you can't find it, please email me at charlotte@charlotte-byrd.com

Wedlocked Trilogy
Dangerous Engagement
Lethal Wedding
Fatal Wedding

Not into you Duet
Not into you
Still not int you

Tell me Series

Tell Me to Stop
Tell Me to Go
Tell Me to Stay
Tell Me to Run
Tell Me to Fight
Tell Me to Lie

Tangled Series
Tangled up in Ice
Tangled up in Pain
Tangled up in Lace
Tangled up in Hate
Tangled up in Love

Black Series
Black Edge
Black Rules
Black Bounds
Black Contract
Black Limit

Lavish Trilogy
Lavish Lies
Lavish Betrayal
Lavish Obsession

Standalone Novels
Debt

Offer

Unknown

Dressing Mr. Dalton

ABOUT CHARLOTTE BYRD

Charlotte Byrd is the bestselling author of romantic suspense novels. She has sold over 600,000 books and has been translated into five languages.

She lives near Palm Springs, California with her husband, son, and a toy Australian Shepherd. Charlotte is addicted to books and Netflix and she loves hot weather and crystal blue water.

Write her here:

charlotte@charlotte-byrd.com

Check out her books here:

www.charlotte-byrd.com

Connect with her here:

www.facebook.com/charlottebyrdbooks

www.instagram.com/charlottebyrdbooks

www.twitter.com/byrdauthor

Want to hear about new releases, free books and get exclusive giveaways?

Sign up for my newsletter!

Sign up for my newsletter: https://www.
subscribepage.com/byrdVIPList

Join my Facebook Group: https://www.facebook.
com/groups/276340079439433/

Bonus Points: Follow me on BookBub and
Goodreads!

facebook.com/charlottebyrdbooks

twitter.com/byrdauthor

instagram.com/charlottebyrdbooks

bookbub.com/profile/charlotte-byrd

Printed in Great Britain
by Amazon